THE LONG AND THE SHORT SHORT OF IT

A COMPILATION OF SHORT STORIES

GREG FIDGEON

COPYRIGHT

Title: The Long and the Short Short Of It: A Compilation of Short Stories

First published in 2017

Address Rock Solid Books, 75 Mountdale Gardens, Leigh on Sea, Essex, SS9 4AP.

ISBN 978-1-9997938-0-7

Book design: Greg Fidgeon and Colette Mason

Cover design: Abi Lemon

Editing: Greg and Harry Fidgeon

For Big Greg and Little Greg

CONTENTS

A BIG THANK YOU...

...**To my beautiful wife Helen** and **my boys Harry and Jacob**. In the words of Bryan Adams – everything I do, I do it for you. Thank you for your love and support. I love you so much. Hugs, kisses and bottom squeezes.

...**To my dad Graham and brother Harley** – the two men who have helped shape the man I am today. **To my mum Doreen**, who brought me into this world but sadly couldn't stay too long to enjoy it with us. Also **to the rest of my family** – aunts, uncles, nieces, cousins, second cousins, second cousins once removeds, in-laws and all the wonderful people I'm related to.

...**To my old crew at the YA** who introduced me to and encouraged me in the world of short story writing almost 20 years ago. **Especially to Steve Neale**, who continues to coax, coach and critique my work to this day over a beer or two. One day the gold will shine for all.

...**To my friends Chalky, Jon, Neil, Stu, Matt, Keith, Mikey, Wellsie, Bushy** and any other individual who has had an impact on my life but I have forgotten to mention. You too have helped shape the goofy idiot I am today and for that I am grateful.

...**To business guru Dan Meredith** for the sharp kick up the backside and for allowing me put some of his life into one of my stories. **To brain wizard Leah Butler Smith** (aka Gandalf of Essex) for delving into my mind and helping me find some clarity. I'm forever indebted. **To John Cusick**, the old primary school friend who believed in me when he had no need or reason to. To **Shari Teigman** for her guidance and encouragement. **To Colette Mason**, the book-publishing hero and fellow metal head. Thank you for your help, support and knowledge.

...**Lastly, to you the reader**. You don't know what you've let yourself in for.

MERRY-GO-ROUND

had drunk about half a bottle of red wine, at least six cans of lager and a further eight glasses of Alan's punch. Not that I'm trying to make excuses, just telling you what happened.

Most of the others at the party were also highly intoxicated. Dave had performed his usual trick of downing a pint in less than five seconds and then led the conga through the lounge and out into the garden where several of the guests, including my wife Sandra, were enjoying the evening air and smoking the largest joint I had ever seen.

"Just going for a piss," I told Sandra, just in case she wanted to know where I was.

I got the top of the stairs to find the toilet door locked and the sound of Peter seeing, for the second time, the meal we had consumed less than three hours ago at the Chinese restaurant.

Luckily, in Alan's delightful three-storey property, there was a second toilet. As I walked up the next flight of stairs, this time having to support my weary legs, I noticed the familiar figure of Nikki.

We had met several times before on this social merry-go-round. I remember having an almighty row with Sandra after one party because I had spent over an hour talking to Nikki when I was meant to be getting my dear wife a refill of that delightful red wine Cheryl had brought back from the South of France.

I denied it of course, said she was drunk and it was more like ten minutes – knowing full well she was drunk and it was more like two hours.

I continued up the stairs and caught Nikki's eye, she smiled and I returned it before putting in an athletic jog for two steps in a pathetic attempt to impress before realising just how weary those legs were.

I got on well with Nikki, I don't know why. I always found something to say when I was with her – the art of conversation is not dead – unlike when I was with Sandra, or anyone else for that matter. She seemed to be interested in what I had to say and vice versa. We could talk and talk for ages; probably a complete load of rubbish but it didn't matter.

But this time there were no words. As I reached the top of the stairs our eyes met again and only one thing was going to happen. I tilted my head sideways and our lips met.

I stood straight and she turned to face me without separating our lips. Now this was not premeditated. We'd not planned to meet at the top of the stairs at 11.43 and 23 seconds. She just happened to be there when I needed a slash, although that had been forgotten now.

I pulled away as I heard a creak. I glanced down the stairs but there was no one there. We kissed again, still having not said a word.

We both pulled away as the toilet flushed. I furiously wiped my mouth in case any of Nikki's lipstick had taken up residence on my face. Nikki smiled nervously.

Gary – Nikki's "and guest" – exited the toilet.

"Awight pal, how's tricks?" he said, completely oblivious to what had just happened.

"Lovely thanks mate, just lovely," I replied surprisingly confident. I hadn't lied – everything was lovely – but I was expecting to say something like, "I'm great mate and I definitely did not just kiss your girlfriend, honest."

"Where's that lovely missus of yours? You best not leave her on her own for too long mate or I'll be in there like a shot, ha!" said Gary. His playful punch to the stomach was stronger than I expected and completely winded me.

I grinned, still trying to get my breath back without gasping like a moron.

"You awright mate? You look a bit pasty." Gary was so considerate. "Tell you what, you squeeze one out and I'll go and crack open another can for us each."

And with that he skipped off down the stairs, slightly slipping on one but regaining composure quickly enough as not to lose face. Nikki smiled at me and made a move towards me. I'm not sure if she saw me pucker up and close my eyes as she walked past me and followed "and guest" downstairs, but I made sure I was just looking and smiling when she looked back.

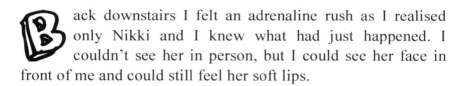ack downstairs I felt an adrenaline rush as I realised only Nikki and I knew what had just happened. I couldn't see her in person, but I could see her face in front of me and could still feel her soft lips.

"Where've you been? You'd better not have been up to no good." Sandra was standing within earshot of others so she had to say it in a light-hearted way. But I knew what she meant was, "You've been longer than I expected, and therefore you're cheating on me. I'll argue with you when we get home."

"He's been chatting up my other half, haven't you mate," said the ever-helpful Gary as he delivered the promised can of lager.

"Something I said?" he asked as Sandra gave me that look and stormed off to bitch about me to Caroline, leaving me to make small chat with "and guest".

He was jabbering on about some goal that so-and-so had scored for England and how he should have got a hat-trick or something.

I wasn't listening. I had spotted Nikki through the hatch in the kitchen. She looked just as interested in what Julie had to say as I was with Gary.

She looked at me, realised I was staring at her, smiled nervously and then turned back to Julie.

"She's a babe isn't she?" said Gary, noticing me smiling at Nikki.

"Yeah mate, she seems great. You're a lucky guy," I replied, quickly wiping away the soppy grin that had covered my face.

"Thanks mate. Anyway, old Smithy goes flying down the wing, past the defender and then hurls it across the box. Well the ball misses everyone..."

Sandra and I left the party before midnight. We were going to France for the day with someone from her work and we had to be at their place by 6.30am so we didn't want to be late in or too hungover, apparently.

We did the rounds, saying goodbye to everyone. It seemed inevitable that Nikki and Gary were left until last.

Sandra gave Nikki a 'hope I never see you again, you slut' peck on the cheek, while Gary broke every bone in my hand with his shake.

I leant forward to kiss Nikki on the cheek, but she turned her head slightly so our lips met briefly. A tingle shot through my body.

Gary spoiled the moment by going in for another friendly jab to the belly, but I managed to get out of the way in time. How I wish I could have just grabbed his arm, broke it and then knocked him out with a punch to the face.

Nikki would then race to my side with Sandra having magically disappeared.

"What are you smirking about?" chief inquisitor Sandra asked as we sat in the back of the taxi. "Oh, just a joke that, er, Gary told me, not that funny really."

I was distracted the whole time while we were in France. I just couldn't get the kiss with Nikki out of my head. I was still away with the fairies when I got to my desk on Monday morning. My boss Kevin had to shout three times and wave his hands in front of my face to snap me out of it.

"Meeting. 1.30pm. Boardroom. OK?"

"Yes Kev, sorry. A touch under the weather, that's all."

And then I drifted back to thoughts of Nikki. And that kiss. I could still feel it. I wish the clock had stopped at 11.43 and 23 seconds on that night so I could stay there forever.

I checked my email; just a few circular messages and poor jokes from my pal Mike in HR, nothing of note. I did some bits and bobs that needed doing, then clicked on Facebook and searched for Nikki Horton. Her smiling face beamed back from the PC and I clicked on her profile. We weren't 'friends' and I wasn't going to risk adding her so soon after the party.

I clicked onto her photos and started to go through them all. A few had Gary smothering her with cuddles I could tell she didn't want, and it got me riled.

"Friend of yours? She's well fit." It was Chris, one of the lads in the office. He was OK, but not really a pal. Still, he asked if I fancied going for a pint at lunch. I didn't.

Instead, I walked aimlessly around the streets of London. Every few steps I saw a woman with long blonde hair and thought it could be Nikki. I got a rush of excitement as I thought it was her and then the crashing disappointment when I realised it wasn't. She didn't even work in London as far as I knew, and even if she did it's a pretty big place.

I returned to the office, tired and depressed. But how that mood changed when I logged back into my PC and found a message from Nikki in my inbox.

It wasn't quite what I would've hoped for. It wasn't a declaration of her undying love for me, a pledge to ditch Gary or a plea for me to divorce Sandra and elope with her into the sunset.

It was just chatting, you know? Asking how I was, how the trip to France was, how fun the party had been in general. Polite stuff.

We continued to chat like this for the next few months, with the odd risky comment in there for a bit of flirting. We didn't see each other in person during that time.

There were social gatherings where we could have bumped into each other, but it seemed that one of the other of us would miss it for some reason. It wasn't deliberate. I made sure I looked out for her. But that's just how it happened.

he next time I saw Nikki was in the park. I was walking my dog and she was walking hers. We got to chatting and strolled round the park side by side.

As we walked, I listened intensely to what she was saying; my eyes glued to her face and lips. Although, I must admit, I don't think I actually heard too much of what she was saying.

I had noticed just how beautiful she was. Don't get me wrong, I thought she was gorgeous before. But I had always seen her at parties when people tend to put in a bit of extra effort to look nice.

This time we were in our civvies, walking the dog. No airs or graces – you can't when you have to scoop up their shit in a bag. But she just had a natural glow and beauty. I think it's only when you get really close to someone that you notice those little traits that make them special.

We walked and talked for ages. As we entered the edge of the woods, I picked up a stick and lobbed it for my dog Beano to fetch. He went after a squirrel.

As we ventured in further, the trees and branches brought a sense of privacy and intimacy.

I asked Nikki about that night at the party and whether she had felt guilty about the kiss afterwards.

She hadn't and neither had I. A sign perhaps that it was meant to be something more? I don't know.

We continued to chat until Nikki stopped. I stopped too and turned to catch Nikki as she threw herself towards me. We kissed, more passionately than before. Again, everything in my body began to tingle. I felt electrified. I felt reborn.

We ended up making love against a tree as our dogs sat and looked on judgmentally.

You'll have to take my word for it, but the experience was much more romantic and beautiful than it sounds. It just seemed so natural, both being with Nikki and being there in the woods.

I told Sandra I was leaving her as soon as I got home with Beano, although I obviously didn't tell her about Nikki or what had just happened.

I eventually had to come clean, just because that's the sort of person I am. I didn't dislike Sandra in any way, really. I suppose I still loved her and didn't want her to find out from someone else.

It wasn't an easy conversation and obviously she was incredibly upset. A few choice words were spoken and a few unnecessary ones from my point of view. But it had to be done, however heartless and selfish that sounds.

Before the black eye and scratches Sandra gave me had time to heal I was living with Nikki in her flat. Gary, by the way, had long since disappeared off the radar. Good job too, otherwise my injuries may have been much worse.

By the time the divorce process was finally completed, the plans for mine and Nikki's wedding were well under way.

We honeymooned in the Bahamas, nipped back to those woods to consummate the marriage and have been wed for three years now.

I went to a party last Saturday though, Steve, a mate of mine from cricket, was having a house-warming do.

As per usual, I had drunk quite a few pints of lager and a couple of vodka and Cokes, but that's not an excuse, just fact.

Nikki was chatting to Peter's wife Dee in the kitchen.

"Just going for a wee sweetheart," I told her. She was probably slagging me off anyway.

As I made my way to the top of the stairs I saw the familiar figure of Jen. I had seen Jen before several times on the social merry-go-round...

GOOD SAMARITAN

at with his head in his hands at the kitchen table Paul stared at the oak effect wondering how it could have come to this. He was just the innocent victim. The memory of that night was so much clearer than any other memory he had ever had.

He went out after work with a few lads from the office for sending-off drinks for Colin. He had bagged himself a major promotion with a huge pay rise, but would have to move to the Saudi office to get it.

The time flew by as the lads and all the other suits in the bar chatted in a mass hubbub of noise, laughter, music and, of course, booze.

Paul didn't fancy going for a curry with the rest of the boys. How he wished he had now. Instead, he walked back to Liverpool Street and got on the train. It was 11.30pm but all the carriages were still busy. He found a seat and quickly fell asleep.

It's amazing how commuters can drop off as soon as the train leaves the platform and wake up as it pulls into their station. The countless stops before were greeted with only a shifting movement of getting comfy again after the person next to them has disembarked.

Paul woke as the train stopped. A quick check to make sure this was his stop and he was off. A few people ran past him in order to be first to the waiting taxis, while others walked fast to their cars or lift home.

Paul was still feeling a little worse for wear and wasn't fully with it. By the time he made his way to the front of the station it was almost empty.

A few deserted cars were left stranded in the car park, no doubt left over night by the owners who would return home drunk later.

He would normally get a taxi from the station but it was only a 20-minute walk. He could sober up on the way, besides there was no one to rush home to.

Without warning, there was a yelp from the darkness of the car park. Paul turned and looked, squinting his eyes to see better. The scream came right from the depths, way past the reach of the street lights.

Nothing. Paul thought about going in but it could be a trick. He hears a girl screaming goes in to find her standing there with three male friends, they kick the shit out of him and nick his wallet.

He carried on walking but again heard a female cry for help. It was different from the last. More desperate, more in need of help.

His heart pounding, he entered the darkness.

He walked almost crab-like, side-on and one careful step at a time, slightly ducked down. His eyes began to adjust to the dark and he saw the flash of a struggle.

He could make out a car with a back door open. He could see what looked like a man who had forced a woman onto the back seat of a car. Him on top of her.

Paul dropped his briefcase and began to jog, still slightly crouched.

As he got nearer, the man stood and turned. He was wearing a black hoodie and wore a Halloween mask. His eyes bored straight into Paul's skull. The man must have loosened his grip on the woman as she began to wriggle free and scream for help. The man turned back, hit her and she fell silent.

Enraged, Paul began to charge at the attacker but he did not move an inch. Whatever he wanted from this, he clearly hadn't got yet.

As the two men collided, Paul connected with a right fist that shook the masked attacker, and the pair fell to the floor.

The two rolled around on the cold concrete floor, occasionally getting in a swipe at one another but nothing significant. Then a car engine roared into life.

As Paul looked up he dropped his guard and was head-butted square on the nose. Pain seared through his face and he felt the warm blood pour out. The woman sped off in the car, out of the car park and off to safety – hitting Paul's briefcase on the way.

"Now look what you've done," said the hooded attacker through gritted teeth. "You'll fucking pay for that."

The two continued to exchange blows and once again ended up on the floor, neither getting the better of the other.

A screech of tyres that burst out near the entrance to the car park spelled the end of the bout. The blue flashing lights of the police car lit up the area. As Paul lay grounded, his opponent upped and fled through a hole in the fence, across the train tracks and into darkness.

The woman was never traced, but it must have been her who called the police. Paul remembered his pal telling him many women don't report sex attacks and rapes as they don't think they'll be believed. Maybe that's what happened here.

A week later, Paul was leaving his house to go shopping when he found a note left under the windscreen of his car. It read: "I know where you live. I told you I'd make you pay and I will."

He called the police and a couple of days later an officer came to the house to speak to him.

"Try not to let it worry you sir," the copper said. "We obviously will put this with the allegations over the incident at the car park. We are hopeful the alleged victim will come forward to help us with the enquiry and we can catch whoever is responsible. He won't keep this sort of thing up. Increases the chances of us catching him."

'Don't worry?' thought Paul, 'Easy for you to say'.

But similar notes were left on a weekly basis for the next couple of months. Paul became paranoid every time he stepped out the front door. Was that guy in Tesco looking at him funny? Is that car behind driving too close?

His only escape from it all seemed to be his Sunday morning football. After a 6-3 win and a couple of pints in The Saddlers, he returned home.

As he walked into the kitchen he was hit by the cold draught. The window was still closed, but the glass had gone. Broken shards covered the worktop and sink.

Paul dropped his football bag and began to search the house while dialling the cops on his mobile. It didn't take long for him to find the message.

A photo of Paul was stuck to the lounge wall by a carving knife. The picture had been taken that morning during the football match.

Why wouldn't this monster let it go? How could it end?

Detective Inspector Colgan asked Paul if there was someone he could stay with for a few days where he would feel safe. There was one person.

"How you feeling pal?" asked Dave, his best friend for so many years until the falling out. But at this time, Paul could think of no one else he would feel safe with.

"Yeah, OK. Thanks. Are you sure Susan doesn't mind?" Dave didn't reply. His face said it all. The affair had been brief, but the damage lasting. Despite their many years of close friendship, Paul had agreed to stay away and he had kept his side of the bargain. Until now.

Dave closed the door and headed to his own bedroom. Paul stared at the ceiling. He hated the feeling that this hooded goon had gotten into his home and now had the better of him. He needed his rest if he was to come back fighting though, so he switched off the lamp by the side of the bed and tried to get some sleep.

Paul was woken in the middle of the night by the scream of a woman. He leapt up in a panic and ran downstairs in just his boxer shorts.

"I told you not to let him stay here," he heard Susan say from the kitchen. He went in and saw Dave cuddling his tearful wife.

"You'd better take a look at this," Dave said. "And then I think you'd better leave pal, we don't need this."

"You can't hide. You can't hide." DI Colgan kept repeating the message scrawled in what looked like blood on the kitchen wall. "I think you're going to have to stay with us Paul. Unless you know somewhere else you could go and be safe?"

"I want to go home, I don't want this bastard to beat me," Paul said. He wanted all of it to be over. He wished he'd never got involved.

"This is no time to play the hero Paul," said the detective, quickly realising what he had said as Paul glared at him.

"I want to go home."

"OK, I'll arrange for a 24-hour guard for you."

Paul noticed the kitchen window had been repaired as he made tea for himself and the young PC sent to guard him.

"So no wife or kids yet then Mr Grant?" said the PC, trying to break the air of tension. But Paul didn't want to talk. He left the copper sipping the hot tea and munching on a digestive.

He went to work the next day in a bid to try to get things back to normal. But he was soon sent home. He was useless and "bringing everyone down", by all accounts. "Take your time and come back only when you're ready," his boss had told him.

Paul printed out the several dozen email death threats that had been sent to his work account and left. He would never go back.

When he got off the train and went to his car – in that car park – he found it daubed with paint spelling out, 'Can't hide'.

Death threats came in the post almost daily. There were calls and texts from dozens of different mobile numbers, but none traceable.

Paul spent his days sobbing. His brain couldn't be distracted. There was nothing on TV that wouldn't bring it all back; nothing in the newspapers or on the internet.

He just sat and cried and stared out the window or into space. Why me? Why didn't I go for that curry? Why didn't I stay for one more beer? Why didn't I jog for a taxi? Why didn't I just walk on by? What would've happened to that woman if I hadn't gone in? Why hasn't she come forward to help me? I helped her, the selfish bitch. Why wouldn't he just let it go?

"Paul? Paul I'm coming in, OK?" shouted the PC in a clear voice. He forced the door open with a strong foot, but it was all too late.

"He just said he was going for a bath guv."

DI Colgan looked at Paul's face under the bloody water and shook his head. He called Dave and Susan Coombs and broke the news to them. Both were still in tears as the curtains closed around his coffin at the crematorium.

But Dave let out a little smirk as Monty Python's Always Look On The Bright Side of Life began to play. Not because he found the song funny, but because he had finally got his revenge.

WIN OR LOSE

felt the drip of sweat as it ran down my cheek to the point of my stubbled chin, before it dropped to form a dark blue spot on my blue T-shirt.

"Take your time Mike, you've got as long as you want," said Chris in a reassuring voice.

I was one of the first to get this far. A 25-year-old bricklayer from Southend on Sea, preparing to answer the question for £1million.

It was tense. The adrenaline rush I got after correctly answering the £500,000 question had faded. I was now feeling numb and a touch breathless as I faced my fate.

"Remember, if you answer this incorrectly you drop back down to £32,000. You can walk away now with £500,000, that's a lot of money," said Chris trying to keep interest up.

"I know it's not A or C, but I'm not sure whether it's B or D Chris!" I replied, looking for any hint of help. All I got was a giggle from the audience.

I leant forward and took a sip of my drink. Another bead of sweat dripped off onto the floor. I reached back and put both hands behind my head, but quickly realised I probably had large sweat patches under my arms. I took up a catalogue-style thinking pose instead.

"Quite amazingly, you've still got three life lines. You might as well use those."

"I think I will Chris," I said. "I'll use my 50-50 first please."

"Right then computer," he said grandly. "Could you please take away two wrong answers, which will leave us with the correct answer and one remaining wrong answer."

Unsurprisingly, the two answers removed were A and C, leaving me with B and D. No further on from before.

"That's not really helped much has it?" said Chris with a smug giggle.

"No, not at all."

"You can walk away now if you like, or you've still got phone a friend and ask the audience."

I opted to ask the audience, but the poll was a dead 50-50 split between the two answers. Shit. Bastards.

"I'm pretty sure it's D Chris. I'll risk it – D," I said, unconvinced. One woman squealed in the audience. It sounded like my girl-friend Julie.

"Where did that come from?" said the question master, who was becoming increasingly punchable with each passing second.

"It has to be one or the other. I've never had this much before and you can't miss what you've never had, so I'll risk it."

"Is that your final answer? You've still got phone a friend."

I paused. A fifth and sixth adrenaline rush tore through my body and then waned.

"I'll call Omar," I said as the audience rippled with nervous glee.

Chris went through the usual routine with Omar, "The next voice you'll hear…" and all that.

I asked Omar the question and told him the two answers available. Then I waited intently for his response.

"Blimey mate, that's a toughie. Hmm. No, nope. I'm afraid I haven't got a clue, sorry."

"No problem mate." Twat.

Chris was back in my face. "Well, you've now used up all your life lines and none of them have been any help have they Mike?"

No, you prick, they haven't. I wanted this to be over.

"I'm going for D. I thought it was D earlier and I've got nothing to lose, so I'll go for it now."

"Is that your final answer?"

"Yes. Yes it is Chris."

"Are you sure?"

"Yes, I'm sure."

"It's an awful lot of money."

"I know, yep. I'm going for D."

"Final answer?"

"YES! For Christ's sake."

"We'll be back after this commercial break."

Wanker!

hris left to get a drink and returned a few minutes later with that smug smirk plastered across his face. Boy, how I wanted to spread it further.

He took up his seat and got the audience to quieten down again.

"We're here with Mike Ealing from Southend, who has got himself into the amazing position of being one right answer away from winning £1million. Mike, before the break you opted for answer D – is that still your answer?"

"Yes it is Chris."

"Are you sure?"

"Yes I am Chris. Yes." I was getting majorly pissed off, but he kept pushing.

"Last chance, do you want to change your mind?"

"NNNOOOOOOOO!" I yelled at the top of my voice.

"Alright, alright. Keep your hair on," Chris said as he repositioned himself nervously. If he hadn't been aware before, he now knew I was unhappy.

"Mike, you've gone for answer D…"

I waited; teeth gritted.

"…I can tell you that if you had answered B…" he paused for effect, looking around at the faces in the audience… "If you had answered B, you would have…" pause again as a smile creeps further across his face… "won a million pounds but you answered D and you lost it. You dozy twat. I tried to get you to change your mind, but you didn't click you dumbass. Are you fucking stupid or what?"

 stared straight ahead as Julie drove us back down the motorway on the way home. She broke the silence after about 15 minutes.

"There was no need to punch him," she said.

"He annoyed me," I said, still fuming. "He fucking deserved it."

"But you know what Uncle Chris is like," Julie said in her calming voice. "And I told you before Christmas that buying him the Who Wants to be a Millionaire game would be a mistake."

PICTURE IN MY WALLET

la do your dance," shouted Matty Dog as the lads got ready for a big night out, the music blaring in the hotel room and enough Joop! aftershave to stink out a small village.

Ola began to jiggle his lanky frame; slowly at first with a few hand movements and a shake of the body, but soon an extravagant and dangerous routine that saw vigorous spinning, with legs and arms flailing.

Dog, El Capitan, Stowaway and Odd Job cracked up as the dancing dickhead continued with his moves.

The lads, 19 of them in total, had been in Tenerife for only a couple of days and were intending to fully enjoy themselves.

Matty Dog was already slaughtered after having drunk the pool bar out of Bacardi during the day. He and Bushy were the first back down there again that evening as well. Ola was nearly dressed, while Odd Job – so called for his likeness to the Bond villain – was still choosing his outfit.

Andy, who had been given the nickname Stowaway because he hadn't actually paid for his hotel accommodation and simply bunked down on someone's floor, got in the shower while El Capitan chilled out in his room.

It was at least 10pm by the time they all finished tarting themselves up and met down by the pool bar.

Ever the classy one, Matty had been amusing the rest of the lads with his fantastic farting ability. He always managed to find a way of getting the maximum amount of noise out of them. On this occasion he had balanced himself against a wall with one leg cocked like a dog taking a piss so the sound reverberated down an alley.

Once he had run out of gas, the lads departed the hotel for the 007 Bar. They had popped in the night before because someone wanted a Bond T-shirt, but ended up staying most of the evening and making friends with the owners and bar staff.

Even the annoying pair out front turned out to be alright – "Hey lads come on in here and we'll get you two for one on shots."

Well, those two-for-ones carried on for a few hours and the lads were well on their way to another memorable night. Except for Terry. He had decided to stay at the hotel tonight. I mean, who does that on a lads' holiday?

"The band are on at Soul Cellar in a bit, shall we move on?" asked Neil. That had become another nightly routine – watching the live band before hitting the clubs. Neil's a top bloke, too. So off we go.

It's all people our age absolutely having it. All except Old Greg that is. He looks like he's well on his way to getting his pension, but was still part of our gang. Our own Peter Stringfellow figure.

The band come on and they only play cover versions, but we just want to dance anyway so that's alright. And the drinks are still flowing of course. Pints and bottles of Dorada, glasses of Sex On The Beach and before the band finish we're off to Busbys and Bobbys for a proper dance.

Ola got himself in another Dorada, but Matty Dog had eased up by now and was on the water. The rest of the lads were scattered around all over the place. It was easily 3am by now, maybe much later, and a few had gone back to the hotel, some to someone else's hotel – if you know what I mean – and a few had gone for something to eat.

Ola was sure the fit dancer was looking at him so he hung around until the music stopped and the lights went up. Turns out she wasn't and by now all the lads were gone. Or at least it seemed that way; Ola was really drunk and things were a little fuzzy. He decided to go across the road to the McDonald's to get some food to hopefully ease tomorrow's hangover.

"Three double cheeseburgers please." He ordered, paid and departed, tucking into the first burger as he staggered back to the hotel.

"Hey hey, I give you nice price. Oakleys, Ray Ban. Cheaper than Asda price. Hey Del Boy, you look." The African street traders were out in force as they were every night and day. Ola just ignored them and carried on scoffing his burgers with a polite, "No thanks."

"Hey, you look at my watches," said another.

"No thanks mate, got one," Ola replied. But this guy wouldn't have it.

"No, you look," he said, grabbing Ola by the arm and pulling him round. Pissed off, but not wanting confrontation, Ola pulled his arm back and glared at the guy before walking on.

As he got to the corner he saw a couple of young English lads, all drunk and laughing at one another.

"Mind your pockets lads, those Looky Looky Men are grabbing hold of people tonight," he said by way of warning and then instinctively checked for his own wallet in the back pocket of his trousers – it was gone.

"That fucking bastard nicked my fucking wallet," he said out loud as he ditched the last of his McDonald's and began to march back to the main strip. He didn't know what he was going to do, but went past the two lads again.

"You and you come with me, I need back-up," he said. The kids looked little more than 16 so goodness knows what use they would be. Wisely, they stayed put.

Clearly the booze had injected into Ola an extra level of bravery and sense of invincibility. He was very tall, but also very skinny. And he hadn't had a fight since second year seniors. And he had lost that.

He walked straight up to a group of about eight street sellers and announced: "One of you has got my wallet and I want it back."

They turned to him slowly, not saying a word. Then a man not much shorter than Ola's 6ft 5in frame stepped forward.

"You fucking motherfucking racist," he shouted, and slapped Ola across the face hard with a backhander.

Ola wasn't much of a fighter. In his drunken thoughts, he assumed that fronting up to these guys would result in one of them sheepishly handing the wallet back and then he'd be on his way.

He didn't expect this. He had never been hit so hard before and stood there in shock while the street seller continued his onslaught.

"Because you're white you think you're better, you motherfucker? Fuck you, fuck you, fuck you." Ola couldn't speak. He stammered but with each verbal onslaught came another slap; front of hand, then back of hand.

Those young lads were right to stay clear. In a way, Ola was fortunate that only one of the men was attacking.

Yet, through the pain, he knew he wanted, no needed, his wallet back. One of the other sellers pulled the man back and Ola spoke.

"Look mate," he pleaded, palms up to show he wasn't being aggressive. "I didn't say it was you, I just said I had my wallet nicked and I want it back."

But it just triggered another attack.

"Fuck you", slap. "Fuck you", slap. "Fuck you motherfucker." This time he grabbed Ola by the shirt and pulled him forward at force and head-butted him in the face.

In an instant Ola was completely sober. He could feel his lips and cheeks were swollen, he could taste blood and his face ached all over. He could feel the tears starting to run.

He looked up and saw the eight pairs of eyes looking at him, the man being held back by the other sellers now. They could see he had gone too far. All of them were very dark-skinned men and their white eyes pierced through the darkness and through Ola.

He realised he had to get out of there. He turned and ran up the road, past the fuckers on the corner who he had thought would back him up but didn't, up the hill and back to the hotel, spitting blood as he went.

The security guard at the hotel only had two words to say as he saw Ola's face: "Fuck me." But he ran on past and knocked on the first door he knew the lads might be in.

"I've been mugged," cried Ola, whimpering.

"You what?" replied Terry. Not seeing anyone else in the room, Ola moved on to his own apartment to find Matty Dog, El Capitan, Odd Job and Stowaway.

"I've been fucking mugged," said Ola again as he burst into the room.

Only Odd Job was there – where was everyone else? – and he sat bolt upright.

"You fucking what? When? Where? Fuck, look at your face. Sit down."

By now, the tears were really streaming and the salt stung Ola's cut mouth.

El Capitan – or Dave to give him his real name – was in the next to come in and the story was translated from sobbing gibberish into English.

Ola went out onto the balcony for some air to calm down.

"What was in the wallet O?" asked Dave.

"About £40 in euros, I took out all my cards earlier. And some pictures."

And that's when it dawned on him. The pictures. That was why he wanted the wallet back even when his face was being relentlessly pummelled.

Inside the wallet was a picture of his mum, who had died when he was just 16. It acted as a reminder. It wasn't on display in there, just tucked behind pictures of his girlfriend and mates. But he would take it out every now and then just to reminisce.

The sobbing that had abated returned and evolved into all-out bawling.

"The picture. It's the picture. I want the picture."

Between the sobs and gasps for breath, Dave managed to figure out what Ola was saying. He passed it on to Odd Job.

"I'm going to see if I can find Matt and the other on the strip," said Odd Job. "You stay here with Ola." And Odd Job was gone.

Dave stayed there holding Ola like a dad holds his crying child. He had only known Ola for a couple of years and now this giant man was sobbing into his chest in a hotel apartment in Tenerife. He patted his back and consoled him as best he could. "Alright fella, let it out."

As Ola sobbed, he thought of what he could do next. Anger started to build. If Odd Job found Matty Dog and the rest of the boys then we would outnumber the street sellers. If they don't give us the wallet, we'll beat the fuck out of them and smash up their stuff. All out fucking war. The rage was boiling now but he knew Dave would try to talk him out of it.

"Could you get us a drink of water, mate?" he asked. But as soon as Dave went towards the kitchen, Ola bolted for the door. He was on his way down the stairs when Dave appeared at the balcony: "Where are you going? It's not worth it mate."

Ola jogged back down the road and caught up with Odd Job as he joined the strip. Matt, Stowaway, Chalky and a few of the others crossed the road at the same time. They explained what had happened and studied Ola's battered face.

"Fucking cunts," said Matt in his typical style.

"It's not worth causing any trouble though," said one of the others.

"There's hundreds of those geezers all over the place. If we start anything, they call out and outnumber us 3-1 easy. Not worth it."

"Looky looky Del Boy." The lads stood there stunned as one of the street sellers approached, trying to flog his sunglasses.

Red-faced, beaten and in a sorry-looking state, Ola stepped forward and spoke up. His rage was gone.

"I had my wallet stolen. It has a picture in it I really need" – he welled up again and took a moment to breathe before continuing – "I don't care about the money, I just need the picture."

"It wasn't a black man who took it, I can't help you," the seller said. He looked back several times as he walked away. He knew where it was.

The lads began searching around the floor and kerbside in the feeble hope the wallet had been chucked after the cash was stolen.

The seller who couldn't help returned, advising Ola to tell the police. He looked up and saw at least a dozen officers walking around.

There hadn't been any cops around when Ola was getting his face slapped like a whore's arse, but now there were loads. He spotted another 30 or 40 sat in riot vans. Had they heard about the beating and arrived to keep the peace?

One of the officers was chatting to a blonde Scottish girl when Ola approached and told him what happened.

"Who took your wallet? Who hit you? You don't know, do you? There's nothing I can do. Go get yourself another picture. What, you only have one and that's it? I don't think so. Go."

Fuck you very much officer.

Ola turned away to see the seller who didn't know anything approaching once again.

"I think if you try and look over there you might get lucky," he said, offering detailed instructions of where to look. Across the road, through the alleyway, and down a flight of stairs behind a restaurant.

"Might get lucky? That's a bit fucking exact for lucky," said Matt with a look that told the seller to now fuck off.

He and Ola followed the instructions and found themselves in a dark and damp stairwell. Although, it was quite probably wet through piss rather than water and it stank.

"You check along there Ola, I'll go down here," Matt said as he ventured further in the darkness. Ola began to move a few bin bags around, hoping the wallet had been tossed behind them.

ucking run. Let's go, Ola. Get the fuck out of here." Matt was shouting as he sprinted up the steps and was then followed by Ola until they reached the relative safety of the seafront restaurants and stopped to catch their breath.

"I went (gasp) down the stairs (gasp) and I saw a wallet on the floor (gasp). I picked it up and (gasp) I looked around and saw about 40 or 50 people down there (gasp) all fucking shooting up (gasp) needles everywhere (gasp) couple of them started to chase me, so I just pegged it. Sorry O."

The wallet Matt had found belonged to an RAF officer. It was stripped of cards and cash, but still had a note with his details on. Perhaps that meant Ola's wallet would still have the picture in.

"It's up to you mate," added Matt. "We can get the rest of the lads and go down there or go and get the police, but they ain't likely to fucking do anything. It's up to you. Don't know if it's worth risking catching anything from those cunts down there though."

They sat there in silence for a few moments as Ola thought. He thought about the drama of the night, getting hurt, the panic, and the anger. He thought about the picture in his wallet of his mum. Then he thought about his mum and her smile and the memories of when she was alive. He realised that was what the picture was for – a trigger for the memories. The picture was gone, but the memories were still there and always would be. No Looky Looky Man street seller could steal those. No one could.

"So?" asked Matt.

"Nah mate," replied Ola. "Let's leave it and go back to the hotel, I'll be alright. It's nearly time to get up again."

THE AWAKENERS

LL night Dan had been tossing and turning. The excitement which had built up over the last few weeks was now turning to nerves. The day was finally here. After about an hour he managed to doze off into a sleep.

"Time to get up son," Dan woke hearing only hearing the last two words of his mother's voice, the rest of the sentence had entered his subconscious.

He wiped the sleep from the corner of his eye and staggered in the bathroom. It dawned on him suddenly that today was the day. Finally The Awakeners were coming to play in his town. Can you believe it?

'Shit, I've to get down there', he thought as he realised he was staring at his reflection in the bathroom mirror with a soppy grin on his face when he should be on his way to Gotten Hall, the auditorium lucky enough to house the magnificent Awakeners.

Dan ran down the stairs hardly touching the steps as he passed them. He may as well have just jumped from the top or slid down on his backside like he used to when he was a kid.

His mum was in the kitchen doing stuff. Who knows what it was she did? She could be an major international drug smuggler for all Dan knew. He was hardly in the house, and if he was he would be locked in his room listening to The Awakeners.

He had the whole back catalogue of their music. The first album *Practise What You Preach* was his favourite. Their second, *I Am Me*, was a typical follow-up. Not as good, but true fans still loved it to death.

He could remember the day his mum and dad finally caved in and allowed him to put posters up in his room.

"What was the point in us paying out all that money to decorate your room when all you want to do is cover it over?" Dad had said every time Dan asked.

But when they said he could, there was no stopping him. Not an inch of wallpaper was in view, all covered in pictures of the band, and many solo pictures of their enigmatic lead singer, Olly Casper.

Dan had once tried to explain to his mum about Olly. "He's really smart mum. He doesn't let anyone tell him what to do, but he's not a complete nutter like some of these other people try to put across they are.

"His lyrics have real meaning; they inspire you and make you want to do something with your life, rather than just accept whatever dead-end existence you find yourself in."

She didn't understand of course, parents never do. They're too old. They never had music like this in their day.

By now Dan was out of the house and on his way to Gotten Hall. It was 11am. The gig didn't start until 8 in the evening but the band would have to turn up way before then for sound checks and everything.

He was smart. No one else would have thought of that. He would be the only one there at that time and would get to meet the band.

"Hey thanks for coming man," Olly would say. "Why don't you come in and watch us sound check?"

"Fancy a go?" lead guitarist Elliott Jarvis would say, offering his instrument to this 15-year-old.

"Woah, you're really good," the band would say as he wailed out track after track from their back catalogue. "What are you doing tonight? Want to come and join us on stage?"

All of a sudden, Dan's spots had all disappeared, his hair was longer, he had a goatee beard and he was rocking harder than anyone had rocked before. Olly sang his heart out as the band gave their best performance ever.

The smirk across Dan's face soon dropped as he realised he was a world away day-dreaming. There were other people at the bus stop and one woman kept glancing at him as he snapped back to reality.

'They probably think I'm a nutter now,' he thought as he boarded the No32 to Gotten Green, 'But they haven't heard The Awakeners. They wouldn't understand.'

On the bus, Dan sat with his forehead pressed against the cold glass, staring out of the window but not seeing anything. He was too busy thinking about the band again.

"You won't want to meet me when I'm dead". The fourth line, second verse from *Back From Beyond*, track eight on the third album *Dream Is Ending*.

'Olly's lyrics are so fucking brilliant,' Dan thought. 'Maybe he's saying that he'll be at peace with himself and content when he's dead, so all those who love him now for his angst and frustrations at the world will not want to meet him when he's dead because all that would have gone.

'Is that it? I'll ask him when I see him later. Olly's so fucking great. The women love him, I love him, not in a gay way, just, I idolise him. I want to be him, just like him.'

The bus reached Gotten Green and Dan got off at Christie Road. He stood and took a deep breath before turning the corner that would put in full view of Gotten Hall.

"Fuck," he said out loud, and immediately apologised to a passing elderly lady, who had gasped in shock at the young man's crude language.

Dan stood and stared at the crowd of about a thousand who stood there waiting at the stage door waiting to glimpse of the band.

He slowly walked forward. People ran past him to get to the mass but there was no point. He wouldn't get to see much of them that far back. They wouldn't invite him in to watch the sound check or offer him the chance to play with the band tonight.

He stopped and sat on a wall. He thought his plan was perfect. How could so many other people have had the same idea? They probably told their mates. Dan hadn't. He wanted the glory of being able to go back to school to say he met Olly Casper and the rest of the band. He didn't want anyone sharing that moment.

But in an instant, his face lit up again. There, walking towards him, was – or was it? Yes it was – Olly Casper.

Olly was wearing all black. Black shoes, black jeans, a black tee-shirt. His hair was blond though, just like Dan's. Even the mobile he was talking into was black.

He didn't believe in commercialised band merch, or designer labels, fake personalities or "fancy gadgets which rot your brain and your wallet" – like an iPhone. Why does he have an iPhone?

"Yeah Ken, hi, it's Oliver," Olly Casper raised his voice to be heard. "Yeah, I'm on my way from the hotel now. The fucking car didn't turn up, I've had to walk. Yes. It's taken about five minutes and it's really humid out here and I'm sweating a bit. I'll look a mess. I'm not happy Ken, not happy. Oh for fuck's sake Ken, there's loads of fucking kids outside the venue, how the fuck am I supposed to get in? They all look like right chavs. Remind me again why I'm playing this shit hole?...100k, right, yeah, that'll be it. But honestly Ken, the car. Someone needs firing OK?"

Olly had stopped about five metres from Dan, who was sat frozen to the spot. But no longer out of awe or adoration for his hero. It was confusion. It must be an imposter, right? A lookalike sent to distract the fans from the real Olly, who would sneak in through another door? But Olly loves his fans, he always says so. Why would he want to sneak past them?

"Yeah Ken, I'm going to go back to the hotel. I'm not going near that lot. Can you call the car people and sort it quick please? And make sure I can get into this place quickly for the sound check. Actually, you know what, why not get Elliott to do my bit for the checks? He's in there already and I can go back to the hotel for a rest. I can get Michael in to do my hair again that way. OK, bye."

Olly didn't even look in Dan's direction as he turned on his heels and went back from where he had come, dialling another number as he went.

"Michael? It's Oliver. I need you again. I went outside and walked for like five minutes...yeah, I know. It needs doing again," his voice fading as he faded into the distance.

'You won't want to meet me when I'm dead,' Dan thought. 'I wish I hadn't met you now. Actually, I didn't meet you. I was a few steps away from you wearing a tee-shirt with your band on it and you didn't even see me. Your biggest fan. You're a fraud.'

Dan went to the gig but it all felt meaningless now. He just stood and stared as the band played and everyone else went wild. He didn't feel angry or upset, he felt nothing. That was worse. The people round him were jumping up and down, head banging and singing along with the band on the stage.

But Dan left before the end.

"So you like the wallpaper after all then son," Dan's dad said as he stood at the door of his boy's room. The posters and pictures of The Awakeners were gone.

Dan raised his head from the magazine he was reading. He didn't say anything, just gave a slight smile. 'Dad wouldn't understand. Parents never do.'

He looked back at the magazine and a picture of Dave Walton from Skull Crusher. Dan had one of their albums and really liked them, and this review of the new one had given five stars. He put his headphones on and connected them to his phone, found the album online and began listening. His head began to nod and a happy snarl crept across his face. Now this is music.

Daily Stroll

ot much going on today. I sat and watched the telly for a while, but there was nothing good. Those people on This Morning did their usual chit-chat on the topic of the day and a bit of cooking. Waste of an hour really.

I had something to eat about midday, but it was pretty tasteless. Always looks so nice on the adverts, doesn't it? Never the same in reality. Still, at least I have food on the table. I shouldn't moan.

It was quite a nice day so I decided to pop out for a stroll. I go out the back door and duck through the broken fence at the end of the garden.

There's a narrow alleyway that separates our row of gardens from those on the houses opposite. It may sound a bit weird, but I like to have a peak over their fences to see what's going on in people's houses.

It's amazing what people get up to, it really is.

The two in the bungalow at No12 are right saucy buggers. She gets kitted up in the old stockings and suspenders while he's handcuffed to the bed. I've seen then with friends round as well for a whole night of fun. I remember one night I was convinced they had seen me looking in as one of them quickly drew the curtains. Spoilt all my fun that did.

The guy at No27 has a stash of dirty magazines in his shed. His missus thinks he's in there pottering about with his matchstick models and model railway trains. Like fuck he is.

He buys the models already put together and painted and just pretends to his wife that he's done it himself. Really he spends his time looking at the magazines and bashing one out over some nude 20-something.

He nearly came unstuck once when one of his young relatives – a nephew or grandson – came down the garden to surprise him.

I saw it all clearly from the alleyway. He was sitting there in his shed, trousers round his ankles with the magazine on the work-bench. His wife sends the boy down from the back door saying: "Go and sneak up on him, he'll be pleased to see you."

The police and social services would've been pleased to see him as well if the boy hadn't slipped on the wet grass. The speed that fella zipped his trousers up! He was lucky he wasn't neutered. Although that's a delicate topic.

There's a nudist family in at No18. Or is it naturist? I don't know. They believe in the "there's nothing wrong with the naked form" thing and walk around with everything hanging out.

But there's nothing kinky about that lot. It's just their way of life. Although it is hilarious to watch them trying to cook without burning their bits. You should've seen it when Kev – that's the dad of the family – tried to do a fry up the other week. He pushed his arse so far away from the hob to avoid the spitting oil that he could barely still reach the handle on the frying pan.

It's not all funny stuff I see though. I saw Mrs Jacobs, the old dear at No30, collapse in her hallway. She was there for about seven hours before she was discovered by her daughter. Well, there was nothing I could do really was there? How could I ex-plain that I saw her fall because I was hanging around her back garden? Plus, I could tell she was already dead in any case.

She was a lovely lady though. Sometimes she'd invite me in for a drink and chat. I think she was lonely and liked the company.

She used to have a cat. I remember calling him No Bollocks. I always believe in calling a spayed a spayed. Haha. It's an old gag but always makes me chuckle, I'm sorry. That cat died too, alt-hough not at the same time as her.

When I finish my walks, I usually come back in home the front way. Although it's right by a main road so it can be a bit hairy getting across without being hit. Those bastards never slow down.

I'm usually pretty hungry by the time I get back, especially since I can't get any food off Mrs Jacobs anymore. Sometimes I grab something when I'm out and eat it on the way home. I've been caught out before when I've just got home and the door's open and I've still got some food left hanging out my mouth. What can you do, eh, when you know it's just the tinned crap at home?

The evenings are pretty dull. Sit and watch more telly. Maybe have a snuggle on the sofa and fall asleep before doing it all again the next day.

It may not seem much, but it's a lot for a little Siamese like me to deal with, I can tell you.

THAT'S MAGIC

Ted Sparrowhawk sat at the end of Southend Pier with a fishing rod by his side and a line cast out into the Thames. The sky was clear and blue and the early summer sun shone down onto the murky brownness of the Thames Estuary. There was barely a hint of a breeze in the air and yet Ted could see the ripples vibrating across the surface of the water, just like the chocolate blancmange his Deidre used to make at Christmas.

He had fished from the same spot at least twice a week for the past 20 years. Possibly longer. And he had noticed the ripples growing and changing in frequency across that time.

They had approached from the East along the river, getting larger and larger for a time, before gradually decreasing in size as if something large was burrowing its way up the Thames towards Tilbury.

Of course he sounded like a mad old fool when he told the other, less regular fishermen who hadn't witnessed this phenomenon.

"Yes Ted, I'm sure the water is vibrating rather than your eye-sight after the bottle of Scotch you have in your tackle box," Edwin Murray would say, and two or three others would smirk and nod in agreement. Mad old Ted they thought.

But he had been here plenty more than they had. And right here, right now he could see it as clear as day – and today was bloody clear. There were ripples all across the river.

He would've picked up his smartphone, filmed the tiny waves and whacked the footage up on YouTube for all to see – but it was 1982 and smartphones and YouTube hadn't been invented yet. So he cursed his luck and washed down his pork pie with a big swig of Glenfiddich.

Sandra Coleslaw had never seen ripples in the Thames; but then she had never fished off the end of Southend Pier either. She had never even been to Southend. She had too much class than that. She was from Barnet.

She was an up-and-coming marketing executive for a City agency and wore a sharp blue power-suit with fuck-off shoulder pads big enough for a jumbo jet to land on. They were certainly cushioned enough to protect her from the ginormous hooped earrings she wore; just in case they fell out and attempted to shatter her clavicle. But we digress.

Ms Coleslaw hadn't seen the ripples in the Thames, but she could feel the odd rumbling coming through the pavement. It travelled up the heels of her white stilettos and into her calves. It had been happening for weeks. Christine in the office reckoned it was a secret government initiative to help people lose weight, like the vibrating belt thing she bought from the mail order catalogue.

But then Christine made a lot of things up. Like when she said she didn't shag Neil from HR at the Christmas party only an hour after getting fingered out by the bins by Gary from accounts. Christine certainly felt the earth move that night.

Neil Inglepot had been thinking about that time he shagged that blonde bimbo with the shoulder pads whose name he couldn't remember at the work do when he was snapped back to reality in an instant. It was a beautiful, sunny day in London and he had decided to take a stroll on his lunch break up The Mall to sit in St James's Park admiring the tits. He never told his mates about these outings though. Ornithology was still not cool, even if that bloke from The Goodies did it.

But that was the least of his worries right now as the cacophony of rumbling and humming sounds that had been disturbing the birds all lunch had now reached its zenith as a huge strip of The Mall was torn apart in a hail of concrete and dirt as a gargantuan spinning steel spike shot from the earth and into the air like a dormant, giant robot's morning glory. The gaping crack across the road grew considerably as a second and then third spike burst into daylight followed by an enormous feat of human engineering.

Neil was only a matter of yards from the first machine, which had now entirely birthed onto what remained of The Mall. It stood at least 150ft high and 300ft long. It was like a building on tracks, but one with a big fucking drill on the end. There was panic all around as City workers and daytrippers ran in fear. Panic on the streets of London. A young Northern lad called Steven looked on and wondered if there was panic on any other major UK cities that day. But then they legged it; accidentally trampling some daffodils in the process. Neil Inglepot, however, was frozen to the spot. And he would remain at that spot forever. The enormous invading machines had begun moving off The Mall and the one nearest to Neil veered left into St James's Park and squashed him under its tracks like a human boot lands on an ant. Poor Neil.

An ageing couple stood at the window of their large detached property and looked out at the mayhem unfolding down the road. The huge boring machines – that's machines that dig through the earth, not unexciting ones – were now destroying the park where the commoners hang out and getting dangerously close to the rather nice buildings on the other side.

"Who is it? Is it those fucking Argies?" growled Phil.

"I don't think so dear," answered his devoted wife Liz. "I think they're busy getting a good hiding in the Falklands. I'd best call someone. Keep watch."

Phil watched as from the enormous holes left in the road – which would be a real bastard on bin collection day, no doubt – came a rolling stream of cars, jeeps, trucks and tanks. A fleet of Panzers came the furthest forward and formed a line in front of the couple's grand home. From round the side came a jeep with a very familiar symbol emblazoned on its bonnet.

Liz joined Phil at the window again as a small man in a uniform got out of the jeep and stood in front of the gates. He swept a hand across his forehead to ensure his greased hair stayed in place and smoothed down his tiny greying moustache. He had been plotting this moment for nearly 40 years and everything had gone exactly to plan. He may be an old man now, but the power and rage still flowed through his veins. Oh boy, how they would be surprised to see him. Awestruck by his resurrection. How they would tremble in fear at his might. This would be his greatest moment. His crowning glory. This would rewrite the history books. His name would go down as one of the...

"Fuck off Hitler you little prick." The voice from the palace was faint but audible. A voice of defiance but not the one of someone in charge.

Frustrated that his moment of glory had been snatched away by such a foul mouth, Hitler raised a loud hailer to his mouth and went to speak again – only for his authority to be undermined by the squeal of feedback.

"Wanker," came another shout from the palace window.

"One more outburst from you and I swear I vill blast a fucking hole in your house," ranted the Nazi, as his equipment finally began working. "From now on, I vill only speak to ze Queen."

"What do you want?" Her Majesty said.

"Zis iz your one chance to surrender. Give me control of your palace, your armies and your country and no one vill die."

A footman entered the room behind the Queen and hurried to her side, handing her a small slip of paper. She unfolded it, read it, smiled briefly, refolded the note and returned it to the aide. Then she approached the window, putting a proud and comforting hand on Phil's shoulder.

"Mr Hitler. As my husband so rightly said, please do fuck orf."

dolf Hitler had dreamed of ruling a new world order since he was a boy on the family farm, spending his days having indecent relationships with all sorts of livestock. He had got his way for so long. The death and destruction he brought across Europe and the world were testament to the righteousness of his vision, surely? But then it all went tits up.

And so Hitler did what every self-respecting psychopath in charge of a country losing the biggest fight in history would do. He tricked his new wife into topping herself and shot a lookalike of himself before burning their bodies and running for the hills. There he would regroup and rebuild his forces to seek revenge at the perfect opportunity. That opportunity turned out to be May 1982 while Britain's military were – if you forgive the pun – preoccupied with Argentine leader General Galtieri's invasion of the Falklands halfway round the globe.

He had been building his new military force from his underground hideaway in the north-easterly tip of France since the fall of Berlin and now his day for redemption had come – but it was being spoiled by a middle-aged woman and her old fool of a husband.

Hitler turned and signalled to the Panzers lined up behind him. The turrets whirred and cranked as they fixed their powerful cannons on predetermined targets across the front of Buckingham Palace. After a countdown of three, two, one they fired at once. Fifteen shells firing over Hitler's head towards the house of the British monarchy. But when Hitler looked up at the Queen in the window, rather than a face of fear and terror, she was smiling. She had seen the odd little man in the dress suit and bow tie arriving just in the nick of time.

aul Daniels had discovered he was magic around the age of 11 when he managed to completely sever half of his thumb, slide it along to the end of his forefinger and then reattach it without pain or blood loss.

As he grew – or rather aged – so did his skill and ability. He was scouted and recruited by a special arm of the secret service in the late 1960s following an incident in which he levitated a young girl called Debbie out of the way on an onrushing train after she fell from a station platform. It was decided they would hide young Paul and his magic in plain sight, by creating a career for him as a popular entertainer.

Now into his 40s, he was the most powerful magician on the planet. Yes there are others, but not at his level.

Earlier that afternoon he had been planning a nice dinner for his beautiful assistant when the emergency alarm had gone off in his study. A read-out on his computer screen told him all he needed to know in three words: "Hitler. Buck House". It certainly wasn't the strangest message to come through over the years. But perhaps it was the most dangerous.

A click of the fingers changed him out of his house clothes and apron and into his dress suit and bow tie. He then stepped into a wooden box, closed the door and when he reopened it he had been transported to Buckingham Palace just in time to see Hitler give the fire command to his tanks. This would be like taking sweets from a baby.

The shells from 15 tanks tore through the air towards the palace. Impact was only seconds away and would no doubt destroy a large part of the building and claim numerous lives in the process – perhaps that of Her Majesty. Paul looked up at the window and saw the Queen smiling down at him. He gave her a little wave and pulled a bunch of flowers from his sleeve. He gestured them in her direction with a little bow and then quickly turned the bouquet into a wand, whispered "Abracadabra" and then fired a huge beam of purple light into the sky that stopped each of the deadly shells in their tracks. With his other hand he lifted off his top hat and then pointed the wand towards it. The shells then broke from their mid-air stasis, flew down into the hat and vanished in a small piff-paff of harmless smoke.

Teeth gritted in fury, Hitler waved at his Panzer commanders again and they turned their turrets towards the little magician. But he just shrugged, smiled, reached inside the top hat and yanked out a 20ft white rabbit.

Hoppy then proceeded to leap over the Victoria Memorial and crush the tanks as flat as pancakes with its huge hairy feet. It then ejected four or five giant brown balls down The Mall that sent Nazi infantry scattering. Paul whistled and the rabbit returned to him, getting smaller with each bound before disappearing back into the hat, which he folded to the size of a playing card and tucked away in his top pocket.

He strode forward to where Hitler stood upon the bonnet of a swastika-clad jeep and the two stared one another down.

The Nazi broke the silence. "You are a very small and peculiar man. You also have very distinct hair. And you clearly have great power. I zink zat you and I have many things in common, yes?"

Daniels smiled and adjusted his white gloves before fixing his gaze back into the eyes of his enemy. "Not a lot!"

When Hitler was a boy living on that farm and playing with all those animals, there was one little piglet he could never catch. It was just too quick and too wiggly. It would escape his grasp and scarper behind a panel or bale and off to safety.

For little Hitler, it filled him with rage. He was used to getting his way. If he wanted Mummy to fix his favourite dinner, then she would do it. And if he wanted to interfere with farm animals, then they would heel to him. But this piglet was insubordinate. It refused its master.

Hitler woke at 2am one morning, crept out of the house and down to the pig pen as quietly as he could. The piglet was asleep, tucked up near to its mother. Hitler pointed his father's rifle as close to the piglet's head as he could without waking it and then pulled the trigger. Vengeance.

The emotions he felt that day were with him again now as this silly little magic man in front of him refused to bow to his command. Rage and the desire for vengeance. He ordered the attack.

A new herd of tanks rolled forward, took aim and began to fire upon Daniels. At the same time, hordes of foot soldiers joined the attack, shooting their machine guns and lobbing grenades in his direction. Other jeeps with heavy artillery weapons emerged from the holes in ground and joined the offence.

At first, Daniels swiped the blasts away with one hand. Then he needed two. Then he needed all his strength and concentration to keep the onslaught at bay. The more he was beaten down, the bigger the demonic smile on Hitler's face grew. He was determined not to give in, but he could now see a swarm of black emerging on the London skyline as the Luftwaffe flew in.

Daniels was in trouble and needed help, but he couldn't reach his hat to pull out Hoppy. And now he was beginning to feel pain as his magic began to weaken under the strain.

The first Junkers began to fire as they flew in over the Houses of Parliament and up The Mall towards Buckingham Palace. The purple orb surrounding Paul Daniels as a force field shuddered under the impact of bullets. And as the first wave began to circle around, a second came in.

But just then, a bolt of fire flew up from within the grounds of Buck House, soared into the air and disintegrated one of the German aircraft on impact. Then a second. Then a third and fourth. Hitler was incensed; Daniels relieved.

He managed a glance behind him and saw his old friend and colleague Ian Botham, resplendent in his England cricket whites, blasting balls into the sky with his bat.

The pair had been on several missions together before. At 6ft 2ins tall and an impressive athletic build, Beefy looked much more of a superhero than his magician buddy Daniels. But now with a little back up and some of the artillery directed at the new arrival, they were both able to give as good as they got. Soldiers were blasted out the way by Botham's balls and Daniels' wand.

If Hitler was pissed off before, he was fucking livid now. His face was bright red with rage and little veins on the side of his head were in danger of popping.

How dare these creatures try to stop his destiny? He would take over this shit-stain of a country and he would destroy all it stood for, even if it meant crushing a few cockroaches on the way. There would be no stopping him.

He signalled for the gigantic machines that had dug through from Dunkirk, under the Channel, along the Thames and up into central London to now move on their new foe.

The huge metal spikes on the front – at least 80ft in diameter – began to turn again as they slowly trundled forward. The Nazis that had fronted the last assault now relented and retreated back behind the monsters now bearing down on Buckingham Palace, crushing everything in their path. The remains of poor Neil Inglepot being dragged along the tracks like a macabre version of the Generation Game.

Daniels and Botham regrouped at the gates of the palace and talked through their options. They were both extremely powerful in their own way, but neither felt they could hold back one of these behemoths – let alone all three.

And then the heavy artillery took up once again. Things began to look very bleak as the full might of the Wehrmacht started to reign down on the heroes.

I nside Buckingham Palace, the Queen had been watching intently as Paul Daniels repelled that insufferable little Nazi. She had called in Beefy Botham as back-up when he started playing dirty. It was clear now that she would need the full force of her secret army.

Celebrities? Entertainers? Only to the general public. Their amazing gifts had been integrated into their respective showbiz careers so that if you saw Paul Daniels lift a car in the street, for example, you would think it a stunt. A genius ploy that kept them and us safe for many years.

Until now, only two had been called into bat – excuse the pun – in defence of Britain.

It was, after all, not very prudent to let your enemies know all of your capabilities. Especially when it came to this level of supreme humans. Until now, the need had been minor. But Hitler was an annoying little shit and was causing far too much nuisance than was necessary for a Thursday afternoon.

By the time the Nazi wanker had orchestrated his latest and most fearsome assault, help was already arriving.

H itler began to cackle as his renewed push on Buckingham Palace got under way. Yes, these two peculiar individuals may have presented a bigger obstacle than he and his commanders could ever have expected, but soon they would be gone and Queenie would have to give up her throne. It was all coming together now, oh yes.

But wait.

Who the hell were these two blokes? These man mountains? Both were enormous in height and weight. One wore what looks to be a giant white mankini and the other a denim romper suit with a fur waistcoat. What the actual fuck?

While Daniels put up a protective force field and Botham tried to take out as many soldiers and airplanes as he could, the wrestling tag team of Big Daddy and Giant Haystacks set about using their extraordinary strength to take down the drilling machines.

Haystacks grabbed hold of the spike on one, bringing it to a stop, and then charged his formidable frame into the body of the beast. Big Daddy went straight for the axle of his machine and used his might to begin lifting in an attempt to flip it over.

Cataclysmic with rage, Hitler ordered a full assault. Every soldier, every weapon, and every vehicle to attack the forces of evil that stood between him and his dream of Britain's demise.

"Thuck on thith you Nathi thcum!"

David Bellamy galloped up The Mall on the back of a 200ft high house spider, which crushed and squished every enemy in its path. Then it set its sights on the third and final drilling machine. Botanist Bellamy whispered instructions to the spider and it began coating the massive drill with its web.

"No, no, no! Who are zeez pipple?" cursed Hitler, his face now an angry shade of purple.

The Nazi and his forces had – once again – completely underestimated the might and spirit of the British. He then turned to see his rear guard being taken out by a new band of bizarre assailants.

Floella Benjamin had wowed the nation's children on Play School. Now she blinded 20 German troops with her dazzling smile and held 20 more in a stupor with her hypnotic storytelling. As more of their comrades tried to fire on the cheerful presenter, their bullets were cushioned and pacified by Flo's foam-filled assistants – Big Ted, Little Ted and Humpty – who she had brought to life. Another toy – Hamble – then froze the Nazis to the spot with her terrifying glare before Jemima the rag doll whacked at them wildly; sending them flying for miles across the capital.

Big Daddy and Giant Haystacks continued to tear apart two of the drilling machines, while Bellamy and his spider had contained the third. Psychic Uri Geller was now on the scene too and was busy helping the trio by bending the machines' metal components this way and that with his mind.

Between them and Botham and Daniels, the Nazi horde was disintegrating before Hitler's eyes. Just like in 1945, the failed overlord could see his dream of occupying Britain was once again crumbling to nothingness.

His mind flashed back to that day on the farm. That piglet curled up asleep. That slight click as he readied the gun. That piglet waking up and running for safety. That shot from the gun that fired into the putrid mud where it had once laid. That force of the mother pig charging into him in defence of her little one and knocking him face-first into a big pile of pig shit. Those red arse cheeks, too sore to sit down on, after his father gave him a good hiding.

And now he had had his bottom smacked again. He had seen enough. He would retreat again and go back into hiding. He turned towards the huge holes that his now defeated and crushed drills had created to flee. But his path was blocked.

he Queen stared Hitler direct in the eye. She was a few inches shorter than her foe, but the crown on her head made up some of the difference. She wore a glorious red cape and held in her hands her ceremonial sceptre and orb. At her sides were two growling Corgis.

She remembered when this monster had previously tried to have his way with Britain and Europe. She had been just a young girl then, but knew full well of the devastation and death he brought to millions.

She also remembered the joy and pride his defeat had brought to the country.

She and her sister Margaret had slipped out of the palace and celebrated on the streets among the ordinary folk. The Queen decided there and then that when The Mall was repaired and the war in the Falklands was over, she would open it up for a street party for the masses. That would be nice. A drop of tea, some cake and some dancing.

Turning her attention back to the menace in front of her, The Queen paused for a second and then spoke to him in her soft but confident tone.

"Adolf Hitler, you are indeed a nuisance. You really are not worthy of the air that you breathe. One is, however, a monarch and one has certain responsibilities and appearances to maintain. The taking of an individual's life personally would be quite inappropriate. Instead, under the powers one holds in defence of one's country, one sentences you to exile from this planet. Goodbye."

A look of puzzlement came over Hitler's face as he tried to take in Her Majesty's words. Exile from the planet? He was equally bemused as she took up a baseball-style stance with her sceptre in hand.

The Queen grinned and grimaced in equal measures as she swung the sceptre with all her might, down low and up, smashing the evil Nazi fucker in the ball – the other, of course, being less than two miles down the road in the Albert Hall – and propelling him at light speed up out of Earth's atmosphere and into the dead of space.

"Now that *is* magic," Paul Daniels bellowed in excitement.

With the rest of the Nazis vanquished, the clean-up operation began. Big Daddy and Giant Haystacks pushed the vehicles, artillery and dead soldiers into a swirling green portal that the chirpy magician had created. Uri Geller began bending the street lights back into shape and casually wiping the minds of the witnesses.

The giant spider had been freaking out some of those looking on, so David Bellamy pulled a matchbox from his pocket and the arachnid shrank down and climbed in. Floella Benjamin had already corralled her little corps and taken them back to the Play School as it was time for bed.

Ian Botham meanwhile puffed on a cigar and contemplated his long walk home.

The Queen called her secret warriors together and thanked them for their strength, intelligence, power and fighting spirit.

"With a swing like that Ma'am," said Beefy, "We might have to find a place for you in the Ashes squad." And with that, they all laughed heartily for several minutes until Prince Philip called The Queen in for dinner.

Ted Sparrowhawk sat at the end of Southend Pier with a fishing rod by his side and its line cast out into the Thames. It was getting a bit dark now and the early summer sun was dipping down beyond Canvey Island; making the Thames water below even murkier and browner.

He looked down at his empty bucket and sighed.

He had fished from the same spot at least twice a week for the past 20 years. Perhaps he should be more like some of the other less regular fishermen in future and start putting some bait on his hook.

Yes, that would be a good idea. And maybe not drink so much Scotch. That would definitely be a good idea. He would do that from now on. Fishing with bait and no booze.

Ted looked over the railings at the end of the pier and down into the Thames. He smiled as he realised he couldn't see the ripples any more. He was becoming more like all those other fishermen already.

PAIN

Your mum's a fucking slag; we've all shagged her," Jamie laughed as he kicked the boy in the stomach again. He then turned and bowed to the whooping from his gormless gang of mates like a world-renowned conductor.

Lewis pulled himself up to his knees, his body aching in so many places from the assault.

"Less of it," growled Jamie as he grabbed his victim by the face and pushed him to the floor, his head banging on the sun-baked mud.

Jamie and his followers turned and made their way out of the recreation ground. They had made their point this time.

Lewis lay on the same spot for about 15 minutes before and elderly lady came past, walking her dog.

"Are you alright, sweetheart?" she asked.

"Yeah, I'm fine. Tripped, that's all. Just resting. Thanks."

He got to his feet and tried to jog away, but the pain in his thigh was too much and soon resorted to a hobble. The old lady knew he hadn't fallen – she had seen those bully boys stomp off – but what could she do?

"You've been bloody fighting again, ain't ya?" said Lewis's mum as soon as she caught a glimpse of him. "I paid a tenner for that shirt and look at it, ripped to shreds. Well, you'll be paying for a new one out of your paper round money and you're grounded for two weeks, goddit? I really don't know what's wrong with you. Now go and sort yourself out before dad comes home."

But Lewis didn't wait up. He went straight to bed to rest. He couldn't deal with dad's questions or mum's accusing looks tonight.

Instead, he lay there thinking about how Jamie Morgan had turned his life into day after day or misery.

Lewis had arrived at the school a year earlier after his parents decided a fresh start was what everyone needed.

His older brother Callum had died of leukaemia a year before and they had all taken it badly. There were too many reminders everywhere – the old school, the old house, the town, everywhere. They needed to move away for the good of their sanity. But it didn't work out quite the way they'd hoped.

Lewis had tried his best to fit in without coming too far out of his shell. But when he won a place in goal for his new school's first XI, it was the first time he had smiled since Callum passed.

He didn't realise, though, that he had knocked the school bully Jamie Morgan down to the second team in the process. It spiralled from there.

Jamie and his cronies made attempt after attempt to injure Lewis in training sessions and when that didn't work, they just began to terrorise him.

Every day they would hunt him down in the corridors, classroom or playground to abuse, taunt and assault him. He fought back once or twice, but there were so many of them that he was easily overpowered. He also found out that they quickly got bored and moved on if he just lay there and take it. Why prolong the inevitable?

But even when he quit the football team and allowed Jamie his place back in the top team, the beatings continued.

It seemed that whatever he did at school, Jamie and his goons would find some way to turn it against him and he had no friends of his own to stand up for him.

The next day at school, Lewis walked into class and found a seat right at the back near a window. He stared out across the school grounds for most of registration and the hour lesson that followed. Mr Capel had long given up on students who didn't want to engage and learn, so he left Lewis to it.

"I'll leave you to it and pay more attention to those who want to be here," he would say.

Mr Capel was now shouting something different. "Lewis Clarke! The lesson is finished and you know you're not allowed in here at break time. Go and play football or something will you."

The last thing Lewis wanted to do was go outside. That's where Jamie and his gang would be. He went to the toilets instead and locked himself in a cubicle. Then came a group of voices.

"I haven't seen that little arsehole anywhere today." Lewis immediately recognised Jamie's voice as he burst into the toilets.

"I saw him in with Creepy Capel earlier, looks like you did some real damage to his cheek J," said one of the goons. They always did their best to suck up to their leader.

"What you doing J?" said another sycophant.

"Leaving my mark. It won't be long till we're out of this place for good and I want to make sure all the new kids know how lucky they were to miss me."

Lewis sat as quietly as he could as he listened to Jamie and his pals smash up the bathroom. Pieces of soaked toilet paper landed on the floor and water splashed over the top of the cubicle, but still he did not move.

He waited for silence. Only then did he calmly make his way out of his prison, glad they had not tried to break open the door. The place was a mess. Water flooded onto the floor from the blocked sinks.

"J WAZ HERE," was written all over the wall in thick black marker along with the initials YIT – their gang name, You're In Trouble.

Most of the urinals were cracked or the pipework smashed up, with the water flowing out of the door and into the corridor.

"What the hell do you think you're playing at boy?" shouted Mr Jones as he inspected the damage. "Thought you'd leave your mark did you? Do you have no consideration for anyone but yourself?"

Lewis had two options. Number one, tell Mr Jones who was really responsible and get a beating of a lifetime. Number two, take the blame and get expelled.

He stood in silence for several minutes, contemplating the outcome of whichever option he took.

"It wasn't me Sir," Lewis said. "It was Jamie Morgan and some of his friends. Oliver Grant, James Martin and a couple of others."

Well, what difference was another beating when he'd had so many?

"Really?" said the teacher. "And what did you do to stop them? Did you just stand there and watch? Cheer him on maybe? Or did you alert a member of staff or tell him to stop? Thought not.

"Would you like this to happen to your house? In my book, you're just as responsible as those who did this and the fact you've grassed up your friends makes you even worse."

"He's not my friend," blasted Lewis.

"Don't answer me back boy. I'll see you after school in detention."

Jamie glared at Lewis as the pair scrubbed and mopped up the mess in the toilets under the watchful eye of Mr Jones. The other boys had denied being there. Morgan couldn't because of his handwriting all over the walls.

"I need to step out of the room for a couple of minutes. Carry on with what you're doing and no nonsense," said Mr Jones sternly, as he turned and left.

"No!" exclaimed Lewis, but the teacher was gone. He looked back at Jamie, who now had a wide, evil smirk across his face.

The first punch knocked Lewis off his feet and within seconds a bucket filled with dirty water was dropped on his head.

"I was meant to take my bird to the cinema tonight," he yelled. "But I'm here with you, you snivelling little prick."

Lewis gasped for breath as the last of the water ran away from his face, but Jamie grabbed him and threw him through a cubicle door. He crashed down awkwardly, ripping the seat from the bowl.

"What's going on? Where's Clarke?" demanded Mr Jones as he burst into the room.

"I don't like to tell tales sir. He's in the cubicle doing something," replied Morgan with a tone a million miles from the angry boy he was.

"Words fail me," sighed the teacher. "Morgan, you may go. Clarke you'll be finishing this by yourself. You came to this school as a very promising student and you've developed into nothing more than a yob."

Lewis didn't argue. He was fed up of the bullying now, whether from Jamie and his band of thugs or the teachers blind to what was happening to him.

He walked home slowly as it began grow dark and chilly. His arms and legs ached from the mammoth cleaning task he had just finished and the mammoth beating from the night before.

e didn't feel the pain until he hit the floor. His legs had been taken from under him by a vicious thug with a metal bar.

"That's the last time you cross me Clarke," hissed Jamie Morgan through gritted teeth. "You're going to hospital for long while."

The second strike ensured the threat was fulfilled. Lewis's leg broke with a loud crack as the metal hit across his shin. He tried to scream, but no sound came out.

He could tell this was different from the previous beatings. There was no gang of crowing morons clapping every punch and kick. There was no one to gain kudos from. The level of violence was more intense. This was pure hate.

Another strike, this time to the head, and there was darkness.

Jamie Morgan was arrested the next morning. He had been seen running from the scene and his gang of louts had turned against him, terrified by the scale of violence inflicted on Lewis.

They told the police all about Morgan's reign of terror against the lad. There was talk of GBH or attempted murder charges.

This made Lewis smile, although those around his hospital bed could only see tubes, wires and hear the beeping of monitors. Lewis could hear what people were saying, but couldn't wake up and couldn't talk to them.

Jamie had said this last beating would end it and Lewis was quite happy it was all over. Morgan would never be going back to school. It will be a long time before he's allowed to do anything freely. He would never be able to punch or kick him again. He would never be able to insult his mother or laugh at the death of his brother.

Mr Capel would never be able to send Lewis out to the bullies again. And Mr Jones would never be able to punish him for being bullied.

He would never have to see that disappointed look in the eyes of the parents still grieving at the loss of their favoured son.

All he had was memories and darkness. No one could disturb him here. It seemed ironic that this place of calm and peacefulness had been forced on him by someone so full of hate, anger and evil.

'I got the last laugh,' Lewis thought as he drifted further into his blissful sleep and never woke again.

TEARS OF A CLOWN

hanks for coming, I'm glad you could make it. Do you want a drink or...no, OK. Let's go through to the lounge shall we? It's a bit more comfortable there.

Take a seat. Get yourself settled. Right, erm, well. I need your help really, your advice. I know we haven't really seen eye-to-eye over the past couple of months but you are the only person who really knows me and, to be honest, I'm cracking up a bit here.

I can't put a finger on when it started, but it must've been after the second series finished. When they said they wouldn't be renewing my contract, well I, I, I, I, I just didn't know what I was going to do.

I'd been at the Beeb since I left university and haven't known anything else. I guess I stupidly thought I had a job there for life.

I've always been a comedian. Well, I've always made people laugh, even when I was a kid. I just can't bear the thought of not being able to do that for a living. What else would I do for a living?

I spoke to ITV and Channel 4, but they weren't interested in me or my ideas. Even Sky, who have been making some good stuff of their own recently, even they wouldn't give me the time of day. I mean, come on. I've won a bloody Bafta for goodness sake.

Now? Well, I think I've been out of the game too long already. People – I mean the people that matter – have forgotten about me.

Things hadn't been going well with Alice before I was cast aside anyway. I wasn't paying her the attention she deserved. Or the kids for that matter. I was just under so much pressure to make that second series a success and to grow the audience that I shut everything out. Even you.

Alice though, who could blame her? A husband who is so much fun on the TV and for his fans, but a grumpy old wanker when he comes home...if he comes home. I can't remember the last time I spent consecutive nights at our place and not at a hotel, let alone when I last took her out or told her I loved her.

When she left, there was nothing really I could say. I knew the reasons why and I knew that if I were in the same position then I would have been doing exactly the same. Sooner, probably. Thank Christ she never found out about the affair.

That fling with Melanie was over before it started anyway. She was just my mid-life crisis confidence boost. A young woman like that taking an interest in an old man like me. I should've seen the warning signs a mile off. We only got together a few times and that was enough for her to see I was a loser and not worth the hassle. Even still I do regret 'overstepping the mark', shall we say, with her.

I told her it was a one-off and it was the drink, but I think she was glad of the excuse never to see me again.

I told Alice that I'd try to sort myself out properly, but she didn't seem to think I was telling the truth either. I know she still loves me and I'm pretty sure I could fix things in the long-term, despite the divorce. I just need to get my ship in order. Get a ship first. I need to stop drinking for a start. I don't even like the stuff anymore. Habit, you know?

Oh dear, look at the state of me. I'm crying now. I'm sorry. 'Doctor, doctor, I feel like a pair of curtains'; 'Pull yourself together man'. Haha. The old ones really are the best...but, I mean, why should I pull myself together if there's nothing to pull together for? You know?

I mean, I can't get a new telly series, I've tried. I'm too old to either start the comedy circuit or those panel shows or to try and do one of those YouTube thingys. I'm washed up. I'm a washed-up, miserable comedian and nobody wants to hire one of those. I can't hide it. What else is there? After-dinner speeches or touring theatres up and down the country for few quid a night? That dancing show? Not with my knees and they'd never have me. Celebrity Big Brother? My goodness, I'm better than that. I'll always be better than that. Bafta, remember?

I remember doing one of those specials a few years back. I had the audience in the palm of my hand. They were in hysterics at every gag, crying with laughter, it was superb. I had such a good time that night. I really connected with the audience and they were absolutely loving it, you know? I didn't want that show to end. I could've stayed there for hours more.

But as soon as the curtain fell at the end and the applause died down, I realised it was over and I had to go back to my sad little life. A quick drink in the dressing room turned into the whole bottle turned into a bottle more in a bar and a bit more of another back at the hotel. All on my lonesome. Just Jack for company. Alice was at home with the kids and I sent anyone else who came to speak to me packing.

I should have seen it coming I suppose; everyone should. It's happened so many times before. Hancock, Barker, James, Morecambe. All comedy geniuses but all miserable and depressed once the cameras stopped rolling, or so I heard.

I suppose it's the same for all of us. The pressure to come up with new ideas and be funny all the time.

'No I'm sorry but it's 2.30am and I've come to the all-night BP garage to buy a loaf of bread and some milk and I've come at this time because if I come any other time I get bothered so much and now you want me to tell you a joke. Well no, actually. Buy the f-f-flaming DVD or look it up on the internet will you?'

Ronnie Barker had the right idea. Just say, 'That's it, I'm off' and then retire to some quiet, isolated village never to return to the small screen. Although even he made a comeback before he passed to be honest. Maybe that'll happen to me. Maybe people will clamour for my return in a decade's time and the Beeb will tell me to name my price. I doubt it.

I could certainly do with that money now. I haven't got the cash to retire yet. The newspapers will say I do, but I really don't. I've spent a lot and, you know, the split from Alice wasn't cheap.

I, I have, er, thought about ending it, you know? Suicide. Mmmm, I have. But, ah, it's quite funny when you think about it I suppose, but I haven't got the bottle for it.

I thought about hanging myself but that seems too painful and open to error. Likewise with cutting my wrists. And I've never been any good at taking one or two Paracetamols for a headache, let alone however many I would need to go that way. Jumping in front of a train? Too dramatic. And with all of them some poor sod would have to find me and I wouldn't want to put that burden on anyone. Well, maybe that prick at the BBC but, you know?

Maybe a hitman is the answer. I wouldn't know where or when then, just pay for hitman to tail me and one day – blam – I'm gone. Knowing my luck they would just bugger off with my money and I'd spend the next 30 years wondering if today was the day.

You may think I'm joking but this is exactly the reason I have called you. I can't see any way out of the situation. No future for this funnyman. So what do I do? I don't know what to do. I can't think of anything. Will you help me? Please?

END OF THE WORLD

ome things in life just cannot be explained and that applies even more in death. I woke just like any other morning on that Tuesday.

I turned my alarm off and leapt out of bed. Into the shower, soap, shampoo, conditioner, towel dry, brush teeth, gel hair, deodorant, socks, pants, trousers, shirt, belt, tie, suit jacket, wallet, train pass, a dab of aftershave and down the stairs and into the kitchen for breakfast.

Coffee, Sugar Puffs, second coffee, check the front page of the paper and then turn over read the sport. Shoes on, grab my briefcase and then out of the flat and on my way to work.

It was a bright and sunny morning. I walked to the bus stop as usual with my eyes down at the newspaper and ears tuned to the sounds of Radiohead.

I stood at the bus stop and waited. And waited. I looked at my watch, it was 8.34am, the bus was six minutes late. I glanced down the road, but it was empty, quite strange for this time of day.

Another five minutes went before I began to lose my patience. Newspaper now in my briefcase, I pulled one earphone out to ask a fellow waitee if they knew of any strike.

But I now realised there was no one else at the stop. Strange for this time on a Tuesday morning. I stopped the tape in my Walkman. Silence. Well almost. Just a slight ringing in my ears from where my music was turned up too loud.

There were no cars on the road, no people bumping and jostling their way down the pavement. No children screaming or birds singing. I was alone.

Confused, I turned and began to walk the streets to work.

I sat at my desk in a state of confusion. I just couldn't figure out what had gone on all around me.

Before today I had only ever seen one dead body before, that of my uncle Col. But on my walk to work today I had seen literally hundreds.

Cab drivers slumped across the wheel of their cars. Business ladies bloodied and bruised from the fall from their high heels to the concrete below.

So much death, so little damage.

I leaned forward and picked up the phone, pressed nine for an outside line and then dialled my parents' house. No answer.

After going through all the numbers programmed into my phone I picked up the directory and began with Mr Aarons. By 1.45pm had made it through to a Mrs Cudson. No one had answered.

Whatever had happened it seemed as though it had wiped out the population of London, at least A through to C in my office phone directory.

I took my tie off – I hated wearing it anyway – and decided to leave work. It's not like anyone would know. I walked past the corpse of Darryl the security guard and through the plate glass window I had smashed to get into the building.

I went over to a black cab that was parked out on the road, opened the driver's door and pulled the body from the seat as gently as I could and laid it on the pavement. I made sure I covered his face with his cap.

Then I headed out of town.

he roads were pretty empty of traffic. Where I did encounter some it was a queue of lifeless drivers waiting at traffic lights. They were now green – the lights that is, not the bodies – but the cars were going nowhere.

I got out of London quickly and before I knew it I had reached St Albans. No life there either. The cab soon ran out of petrol. I found a petrol station but couldn't work out how to use the pump as the attendant was collapsed and useless.

I checked two other cars on the forecourt. One had obviously just pulled in and was also near empty, but the other – a Range Rover – was just about to leave and was primed with fuel.

What I guessed was the driver, a middle-aged man in beige combat trousers, a baggy jumper and baseball cap had fallen before return from payment.

I decided to go home and make some dinner.

A week passed before I ventured out of the house again. I was out of food and needed to restock.

The freezer section at Sainsbury's was still fully functional and I piled up two trolley loads of goods as well as long life milk, cereal and tinned goods. I also went through the magazine rack picking up a copy of everything from Viz to Bliss; a copy of Q magazine gave me an idea.

It advertised a competition to win a trolley dash through HMV.

Having dropped off the grocery shopping at home I made my way to Oxford Street.

The Range Rover proved too small for my spree in the end. I smiled with contentment as I drove back to the flat in a Topshop lorry filled with clothes, a massive home cinema system and thousands of pounds worth of other goods.

I tried not to think of all the stricken bodies I had stepped over or around. It was just something that happened. But I also didn't want to hang around such a populous area.

My journey back to the flat was to pack up the food I'd bought and a few personal belongings before setting out to find a bigger, posher residence. I had free choice of England. I had become the first person to win the lottery without buying a ticket.

I enjoyed the finest wines, cooked what meals I could with depleting supplies, played computer games, listened to music, watched films, swam in my pool, worked out in my gym.

Some days I didn't bother putting any clothes on. Others, I would dress in a full suit, waistcoat and top hat. On occasion I would go fancy dress. I ran across the pitch at Wembley Stadium while dressed as Superman.

I missed my parents, but since I moved down to London a few years ago I had seen them less and less anyway. I had been a worker, primed for a nice early retirement. I had no girlfriend, no real friends at all, just colleagues and acquaintances.

I had little in my life so I had little to miss. I guess that helped me to survive in this lonely new world.

I often sat and wondered how I could be the one man left alive. Why me? Was I picked or was it an accident? Should I be dead? What actually happened? And how did I manage to sleep through it on that Tuesday morning?

As I thought about it, it dawned on me that I may not be the only person to have survived. The world's a big place after all. Perhaps there was someone in the States now enjoying the delights of Disney World for free.

I decided that, actually, the chances of me being the only survivor were slim. That's why I decided to explore a little further afield.

I didn't need to save to travel now. I could sail and would head to France. But not yet. No, I didn't think I wanted company just yet.

If I found people there that would be it, I would have to share my freedom. I wanted a bit more "me time".

t was another two months until I made my way down to the South Coast with the aim of sailing to France. The day before I left I had been walking around Kensington looking for a really nice car to drive down in. A Ferrari or something flash like that.

Obviously I had thought about sex in the many days since that Tuesday, but a supply of nudey magazines and videos and appeased my appetite.

But as I turned into a back street on my hunt for a supercar, I saw the body of the most beautiful woman on the floor.

I had passed hundreds and thousands of these corpses over the months and, if I'm honest, I try not to look at them.

But this girl caught my eye.

She was probably in her late 20s and her face was perfection. She had soft pink cheeks with her golden blonde hair framing it. Her ruby lipstick was unblemished. Her eyes closed as if she were just taking a nap on the pavement.

But as I looked down her glorious body, I realised her fall to the ground had been less than graceful. She was wearing a loose summer dress and the top had been half pulled down to reveal one breast. The bottom had concertinaed up to her waist. She was not wearing underwear.

I don't know if the loneliness had finally kicked in or if I was going loopy or it was just the heat, but I became overcome by lust.

In everyday life, this goddess wouldn't have taken a second look at me. But this wasn't normal life any more. My mind was racing.

I left for France straight afterwards. That kind of behaviour just wasn't me – it had scared me. What would I become if I continued this way?

As I walked away from that girl on that street, looking back to see her dress now covering all it should, I knew I was still a good person. But I needed to find other people if only to preserve my sanity.

I hit the South Coast later that evening and set sail for France the next morning. Conditions were good and the boat I had chosen was pretty fast. The funny thing is, I had learned French to a very high level while at school, but this was my first visit to the country since I had left – and I had no one to talk to. No one I found anyway.

I drove down through Paris, eventually ending up in the South of the country. Then I drove back up again. I continued around Europe for the next nine months and didn't encounter any other living beings.

Food wasn't in great supply. Some fruit and vegetables still grew, but I ate grass and any insects I found. I would pick through chickens, dogs, cats or any other animals I could find which could be edible.

The hunting took time and used up a lot of energy. I remember once being asked by a work colleague of mine – ex work colleague now I guess – if I would eat human flesh if the circumstances left me with no other option. I thought he was a bit of an oddball, and of course said no. But after three months of eating very little I was becoming very thin and very weak.

What human flesh tastes like, I couldn't really say for sure. I covered what I ate in sauces to disguise what I was consuming.

I was disgusted with myself, but I was desperate.

I made my way back to England, using the same boat to cross the Channel. I went the long way round and chugged my way along the Thames so I could go under Tower Bridge while tooting the boat's pathetic horn and waving to the non-existent crowd. The brave explorer returning from the new continent.

Tired, hungry and alone, I returned to my flat. I was bored of the big house, the big TV and all that stuff. Although I had lived much of my life as a singleton, I missed companionship. I missed seeing other people live their lives.

It took a long shower and then a soak in the bath to rid myself of the dirt, grime, sea air and salt from the sea.

One year, three months and 22 days after had woken on that Tuesday morning, I went back to bed.

If the date on my clock was right, I had slept for three days. But however long I'd been out, I woke to the hubbub of daily life. I looked out of the window to see people going about their lives. I was ecstatic. People, buses, life.

I phoned my parents in tears and told them I loved them. I would drive up and see them at the weekend, I promised.

Then I phoned work and took the day off. Over a year off and I call in sick on the first day back.

I'm not sure when everything came back online, but the woman on the news said the 15-month glitch in time was due to a huge and unexpected surge in magnetic forces pulling through the universe as two planets millions of lightyears away collided. It caused the Earth to shudder, knocking everyone to the ground.

No one had died, simply ceased living for a bit. It was as if God had accidentally leaned on the remote control of life and hit the pause button. But missed me out.

There were lots of weird stories emerging in the fall out. People waking up with body parts missing. I ran to the bathroom and threw up. Later, there was a story about a Lord being arrested for theft after a lorry-load of goods was found at his country manor house. A Topshop truck had been left at the property too.

I didn't tell anyone what I knew. Not at that point, anyway.

After a few days I made my way back to Kensington, found the quiet back street and knocked at number 23. A pretty blonde woman answered the door.

"Suzanne Joseph?" I asked, already knowing the answer.

"Yes?" She replied, puzzled. "What is it?"

"I, er, I found your purse. It was in the road. It, um, had your address in, so I thought it best to return it. Funny that blackout thing, how are you?"

"Fine. You could've brought this back sooner, you know. I've already had to ring to cancel my credit cards. Such a pain."

I was taken aback by her tone. It didn't match how I had seen her in my head. Why was she being so rude?

I could've done whatever I wanted to her that day, but I chose not to. I covered her up and left her be. I had taken care of her. Now I was kindly returning her purse, even if I had stolen it in the first place. I snapped. My thoughts burst out.

"You looked so nice and perfect when you were laying there on the pavement. I looked after you when you were naked. I could've done anything to you."

Suzanne put her hand over her mouth as she gasped and tried to slam the door shut, but I stopped it and continued with my outburst. It all came out.

"I've spent the last 15 months searching for someone to talk to. All I could think about was you. I've eaten human flesh just to stay alive to get back to you. I did it for you. Why are you being so horrid?"

I collapsed in a heap on her doorstep as tears flooded down my face. It was the first time I had cried since I was a child. Suzanne slammed the door shut and called the police. Her neighbours began to stare through their windows. But none of them could understand what I had gone through. They couldn't understand what I was still going through. I had lived in a world with no people and now they were all back I was lonelier than ever.

I said nothing as I was placed into the back of a police car. The officer told me to mind my head as he guided me in. I was questioned as to how I came to know of Suzanne and what I was doing there.

My explanation did not make for good hearing. But I was tired of being the only person who knew. Swabs were taken and the contents of my stomach and intestines checked. The investigation into my actions went across Europe.

My legal team advised me to go for an insanity plea to get the shortest prison sentence possible but I declined. Now my life is paused again and I can begin to sleep in peace.

HEROES AND VILLAINS

HE argument was inevitable. The only surprise was how long I had managed to bite my tongue before I finally snapped.

Dad and I hadn't seen eye to eye for a long time, but he had now just become a bitter and spiteful old man who took glee from making others unhappy. I had told my mother to leave him and come stay with us on numerous occasions. But she always insisted he was as sweet as the day she met him and that we just brought the worst out in each other. I found that hard to believe.

She was a very traditional woman – the housewife who raised the child, kept the house tidy and made the dinner while husband earned a crust – and divorce would not enter her mind.

My rift with Dad started to grow in my late teens. For his many, many faults he was clever and a brilliant businessman. As a young man he had invented an ergonomic handle for hammers. He patented the design and began manufacturing it and other similar hand tools. Then, as DIY got something of a boom in the 1970s, he released a series of 'how to' books and the Jackson name really took hold.

More tools followed – from electric screwdrivers to use around the house up to plant machinery – and the family name became a staple of toolboxes across Britain. It was known for usefulness and reliability. "Jackson's is trust," was the slogan.

Nowadays you can't move in a B&Q, Homebase, a Wickes or the trade outlets without seeing displays with Jackson's products. As well as the tools, there are also work clothing ranges, boots, cups, and even associated children's toys to groom them into the brand young. Dad was a multi-millionaire and all from a business he started in his shed. Mum had been at his side the entire journey. She would easily take half his fortune if she left, as I often told her.

Dad had plans for me, his only son and heir, from a young age. After leaving school I would serve a three-year apprenticeship at Jackson's – one year on the manufacturing floor, one in research and development, and a third in the admin and HR side of things. Then I would be ready to take a senior management position and a position on the board, with the aim of taking over the running of the company if and when Dad wanted to step away.

The problem was it wasn't what I had planned for me. I inherited my mother's talent for art. I loved to draw. And that was the avenue I wanted to go down. Dad saw it as a betrayal. He begrudgingly allowed me to go to university to study art thanks to a lot of persuasion from Mum. I could tell he was fuming underneath it all. He insisted that I try to focus on the aspects that could help the business in future; designing new tools or whatever. But my passion was in illustration. Drawing characters and scenery. I had no intention of ever working for Jackson's unless they launched their own version of Bob the Builder.

I launched my first series of graphic novels while I was at uni. I also set up my own graphic design business to take on clients who needed and appreciated the skills of an artist. It helped to keep my debts down and my social life active.

Whenever I went home or my folks came to visit, the only thing Dad would ever really say to me was, "How's the comics?" The word 'comics' fell from his mouth like he was allergic to it – like he was doing all he could to stop from heaving. Mum would just sigh and try to change the subject. I would tell them about a big cheque I'd just got in or a deal I had signed, even if it wasn't true. I never once asked Dad for money, despite my mates urging me all the time. "Think of the nights out we could have." Perhaps that irked Dad; that I never went to him for help. I wasn't really that bothered. But there was always friction and an argument just below the surface, waiting to burst out.

Dad had grown up in the East End of London and was a fan of West Ham football club. I didn't like football that much, but I still bought a Tottenham Hotspur shirt just to wear when I visited him. That really wound him up.

He also loved his cricket and had pictures of Gower, Botham and his other England heroes on the walls of his office. So I followed Mum's heritage and started supporting the West Indies, just to go up against him. I didn't really like cricket either; rugby was my sport but Dad had little interest in that. Maybe that's why I chose it. My art and my rugby against his business empire and his cricket.

I felt sick with guilt as my final year at uni came to an end. It was coming to crunch time and I knew Dad would be unbearable once he knew his crown prince Charlie didn't want to take his throne. The guilt was for leaving Mum to deal with the fallout. By this stage I couldn't give two shits what Dad thought. But I wasn't going to hang around to find out. I lied to them about when I would finish uni and a week before I sent them a letter explaining my feelings.

"Thank you for the opportunity, I really do appreciate it Dad. But I want to be my own man, make my own mistakes, earn my own money and be my own success in a space that is far removed from your own. I know this will be hard, but please try to understand. Your son, Charlie."

As it turned out, he didn't understand.

I had set off on my travels immediately after sending the letter. I actually posted it from the train station. My graphic novels had a decent enough following and I was able to sell art as I went as well to help cover the costs. The freedom I felt was amazing. No one to answer to, no expectations; just living life day-to-day in some of the most extraordinary places in the world.

But then, somehow, Dad tracked me down to Goa and we had a massive stand-off on the beach.

It was quite remarkable really. The sky was a crisp blue, the sea clear and beautiful, the sand golden, the trees showing a brilliant shade of green – we were in paradise. And yet we shouted at each other for at least half an hour without a second thought for our surroundings. The locals stared at us like we were crazy, while some of the tourists looked on like it was a soap opera.

He said some harsh things and I said many more worse back. Then he issued the ultimatum. You can probably guess what it was. "Return to England with me now and take your place in the company or else I will cut you out of it forever. You will not, re-peat, not be able to skulk back in a month, a year or a decade and say 'Dad, I've changed my mind'. Now, do you understand?"

Ouch. That last bit. He used the words from my letter against me. But I did understand. Like the waters lapping yards from our feet, it was crystal clear. "Bye Dad."

It was while I was in Goa that I met Mia. There were loads of us who were travelling who hung out at the same places and after a few weeks we had formed a family of assembled friends from all over the globe.

But I didn't quite realise how much of an impression Mia had made on me until I left for Thailand a month or so later. Yes, I'm fully aware that I wasn't too original in my travelling destinations.

Fortunately, Mia did realise there was something there and man-aged to scrape together enough money to follow me to Ko Samui and find where I was staying. She's tenacious that girl. She was from Durham. I loved her accent. I used to call her the posh Geordie and each time she would take the bait and snap back,

"I'm no a Geordie." She was so pretty. So much fun. So easy to be around. So perfect.

We kept on travelling for nearly another year before we decided that we wanted to return to England and set up home. It was time.

Mum and Mia had spoken on the phone a few times and got on well. They really hit it off after we got back and they both did a lot of the legwork in finding us a good spot outside London, but not too far so we could commute in.

Mia was a teacher and hoped an inner-city school would jump at the chance of taking her on despite her disappearance around the world after university.

Mum had told me Dad did not want to see me. I didn't expect anything else. I also didn't expect the letter he sent just after we moved in confirming his previous stance still was still in place.

"Please be aware that there is, nor will there ever be, a position within the Jackson business for you. You made your choice. I grant your wish and will allow you to make your mistakes, but know that I will not be there to pick up the pieces."

The letter even had a printed signature – he hadn't even taken the time to sign it himself.

My reply was a certificate from the Deed Poll office, notifying him that I had changed my surname to that of Mum's maiden name. I was now Charlie Reid. There was now no heir bearing the Jackson name.

You will have guessed that there had been some thawing in the relationship to get us from the point of me disowning the family name to being in his company for this most recent row to occur.

That thawing came when Mia fell pregnant with our son Oliver. Mia and my mother were already close, but this brought them closer and they spent more time together, what with Mum not having much to do each day other than housework and cooking.

We found ourselves in a cycle. Dad and I would not be speaking for about three months. Then we would end up in a room with one another and exchange pleasantries but never apologise for the previous row. At some point later, Mum and Mia would convince us both that dinner or a get-together would be a good idea. Said get-together would be held and at some point Dad and I would argue furiously. Then we would not speak to one another for about three months. And off we go again.

Fortunately – well, that depends on how you look at it actually – one of the "get-togethers" was mine and Mia's wedding. It was good in the sense that we were on civil enough terms for me to invite Dad and so not to put Mum in an awkward situation.

But it meant that the row came during the reception when he made a comment about the quality of the food. "You really do get what you pay for, don't you?" he said smugly as he tossed a sandwich he'd taken a bite out of back onto the buffet tray. It ended with him paying for a taxi back to his hotel.

He had made similar comments to cause the row tonight. In fact, I think today he was worse. He said to Mia that he had read her school's Ofsted rating had fallen from Outstanding to Good. We didn't live in the same borough, so it's unlikely he would have read it in the local paper. He would've had to go out of his way to find something like that out. That's how devious he had become. All that effort just so he could embarrass Mia in front of everyone and rile me up.

"Kids are kids are kids," he said. "They're the same all over the country, so the failing has to come down to the quality of the teaching, doesn't it?"

Mia was too nice a person to argue back to her father-in-law. She just said how difficult the situation was for everyone at the school due to funding cuts.

I told him he was a nasty prick and a bully. Then I told Mia to get her coat, Oliver to pick up his Iron Man toys and Mum that I was sorry, but I can't handle his bullshit.

"This is why I didn't want to come round on Christmas Day, because I knew he'd spoil it with shit like this just like he always does. Merry fucking Christmas. Why don't you make a New Year's resolution to stop being such as wanker, eh dad?"

He didn't even take his eyes off the telly; just supped at his pint of ale with a small, victorious smile on his face. See you in three months, arsehole.

Luckily, Oliver didn't pick up on the choice new words daddy had used towards Grandad this evening. Or at least he never let on if he did. He was six and obsessed with superheroes and – nothing to do with me – football.

I gave him a piggy back up the stairs to his bedroom and then read him a book we got from the library; one of those short ones where every other line has to rhyme. I tucked him in under his Avengers duvet, stroked his forehead and then made sure he had his cuddly Hulk toy to snuggle up with and keep him safe.

"Dad?" His brow was furrowed, which showed he had really been thinking hard about the question that was to come. I hoped it wasn't about why his Grandad was such a twat; we'd be here all night.

"Yes son?"

"Are superheroes real?" It caught me off guard.

"Well, er, there are doctors and nurses and firemen who save people's lives every day and rescue people and police who arrest bad guys…"

"No, I mean people with superpowers."

"Mmm, not that we know of, no. But we've never met any aliens and they could still be real."

"They're not." Oliver said this with stone-faced certainty.

"Oh. No?"

"No. Alexander Harvey at school said."

"Ah, OK. And he would know wouldn't he?"

"Yes. He's clever. So there are no real superheroes then? They're just made up like in your comics?"

"Graphic nov...um, no. No Oliver. I don't think there are."

"I hope there's no villains then." And with that he rolled over with his eyes closed ready to sleep.

'Oh, I'm afraid there's plenty of them,' I said to myself as I switched out the light and shut his door.

It was late, so I got into bed. Mia was in the bathroom. I opened up Facebook on my phone and scrolled through the feed. A few people ranting about politics; I didn't like to get involved. Some people doing that naughty elf thing for their kids; I didn't want to get involved. A funny video; I couldn't be bothered to watch it. Brian Tuckey's house had been burgled while he was out for dinner. All the kids Christmas presents were gone. The telly too, and some cash and his wife's jewellery. Comment: "Bastards. Sorry Bri. Let me know if there's anything I can do." I knew there probably wasn't, but it's polite to say something.

As it would turn out, Brian's wasn't the only house to get burgled in the days leading up to Christmas. I knew two other people personally and there were reports of four others in the paper. And it wasn't tip-toey stuff in the dead of night with a guy holding a bag marked 'swag' either. It was a gang knocking on doors and threatening whoever opened with a pistol. Real or not, it must have been terrifying. And 30 minutes or so later, once their van had been filled, off they went.

Fortunately, there hadn't been any casualties other than a few blokes getting a bit of shoeing after they tried to defend their families and their homes. But Christmas for them – and quite probably a normal life for a long while afterwards – was ruined.

The home insurance would probably replace or cover the cost of the stolen goods, but it can't fix the mental stuff.

I got back out of bed and checked the front and back doors were locked, taking a look down the road too in case of any white vans lurking about. Not that there was much to nick from our place. I only had a couple of regular clients for my design business and my graphic novels weren't doing so well. It's ironic that in an age where superheroes are so huge in cinema and in toy shops, people are still afraid to take a chance on novels that don't feature the mainstream characters.

My best-seller had been The Chronicles of Ace Stone, a former SAS soldier scarred by the horrors of war. He has turned his back on weapons and embraced the martial arts. Disenfranchised with modern society, he lives in woodland and forages for his food. But he returns to the city at night to take down the thieves and hoodlums who terrorise ordinary folk. And he has had love inter-ests, long-term nemeses and sidekicks, and loads of great storylines but we won't go into all that now. It's not important.

What I was saying was that it was only a moderate success. It helped cover some of the bills at least, but the time put in wasn't really rewarded. A film production company did once pay me a couple of thousand pounds to hold the rights for a year, but they never did anything with it and no one else has shown any interest since. Most of my time I sell a hundred or so copies a month.

I was considering, for the first time, taking on a "normal" job. Obviously not with the biggest local employer though. But this spate of robberies had given me a good idea for a future Ace Stone storyline. Well I say idea, I was going to steal the whole set-up. Most of the time the best stories come from real life.

Mia smiled when she saw me writing in the notebook she had bought me in Thailand all those years ago. It was getting really tatty and full up now; crammed full of years of ideas for stories and characters. I would need a new one soon – maybe she's got me one for Christmas. Mia turned out her bedside light and snuggled up alongside me; rubbing her hand up and through the hair on my chest. Then she slid it down across my stomach and into my boxer shorts. Woah. It seems Christmas had come early and it wasn't a notebook I was getting.

I slept very soundly that night. Content. Happy. Loved. It was gone 1am when something woke me. A faint humming sound. Not sure. I was confused, still half-asleep. Then I realised it was my mobile phone vibrating on the bedside table next to me. Squinting into the bright light of the display, I was now even more confused.

'Dad calling...'

I drove across town as quickly as I could without being a complete idiot. My heart was pounding nonetheless. The call from dad had been bizarre and heartbreaking. He had been out for the evening at a Jackson Ltd board members festive dinner. Mum would normally go with him, but she had been feeling under the weather and didn't want to be ill over Christmas itself and so she had stayed at home.

Dad's driver had been unable to operate the electric gate when they arrived back and they later found it had been jammed. My parents' house is very large and set a way back from the main road. But Dad could still make out a white van parked at the side. He called Mum's mobile and she only managed to tell him there were four masked men in the house before one of them grabbed the phone.

Dad said he heard the sound of a hit or slap and then Mum whimper. I welled up instantly, both in anger and despair.

He had called the police and then me. He was going to go into the house to challenge the intruders, but was stopped by his driver.

When I got there, the front gate was surrounded by police. At least five cars with their blues flashing round, but all the officers were outside the property. I told one copper who I was and was taken up to see another officer who was "leading the operation". I gave it the bunny ears because he stood there drinking a cup of tea having taken the decision to wait for the robbers to make their demands.

"They will be able to see they cannot get out. And seeing as Mrs Jackson is inside, this has now become a hostage situation. We have some specially trained negotiators on the way but, as you will appreciate, they are not always nearby. But they will be here soon and then we will make contact with the suspects," he explained.

"What's your name officer?" I asked.

"Chief Superintendent Christopher Howerton."

"OK Chief Superintendent Howerton. This has only become a fucking hostage situation because your officers are barricading the only exit those bastards have got. If you all fuck off, they will too and hopefully without hurting my mother. Understand?"

"I appreciate these are difficult circumstances Mr Jackson…

"…Reid. Charlie Reid."

"..Oh. I thought...never mind. As I was saying, I appreciate these are difficult circumstances but these are very dangerous men inside that house and we have an opportunity to apprehend them tonight. If, as you suggest, we let them go, they could carry out multiple other attacks. Or we can nip it in the bud. I said the same thing to your father when he wanted me to storm the house at once."

"That's because my mother is in that house with men with guns. If you….."

I bit my tongue. I wasn't going to waste any more breath on this wanker and walked away before I ended up in the cells for Christmas.

Where was Dad anyway? I could see at least a dozen cops and a handful of neighbours had come to the end of their drives to gawp. I saw his driver Pavel and made my way over. It took him a second to work out who I was. It wasn't like we saw each other that often and not in the state I probably looked now. He said Dad was in the back of the car; a V-Class Mercedes-Benz, which was basically an expensive people carrier. Dad liked shepherding people about in it, whether that be business associates going for a game of golf or friends going for a night out. It had blacked-out windows at the back, so I couldn't see the miserable old goat inside. I was still none the wiser when I opened the sliding door and looked inside.

"He's not in there Pavel," I said. Pavel just looked gormless and shrugged. "Shit."

I pulled my phone out and there was a text from Dad. I hadn't felt it vibrate. The message said that he was in his work shed out the back of the house – what the hell was he doing in there? – and told me to come meet him.

The route he instructed me to take involved going through next door's garden. That may seem simple, but his next door isn't the same as mine and yours. From door-to-door – going down one driveway, along the road and then up the other – it would take you a good ten minutes to walk. These are very wealthy people remember and these houses, well mansions really, were enormous.

I pretended to chat into my mobile as I walked past the coppers by Mum and Dad's front gate. Next door's was similar in that it was about 10ft high and had spikes on the top. The design was quite poor, though, as the ironwork offered a foothold near the top that allowed you to step over the spikes without catching the family jewels.

Once over I stayed close to the inside fence that ran alongside my parents' garden. I had to go through a gate into the next door's yard but fortunately it had already been bashed open, presumably by Dad. A security light came on once I reached the back garden, but it proved to be a help as at the rear end I could see my father frantically waving me towards a hole he had created.

"Dad, what the fuck are you doing?" I asked as I ducked through some hedges into my parents' garden. Dad shushed me and jabbed an old wrinkly finger towards his shed.

Again, like the house and the "next door", this wasn't like a shed you or I would have. It was pretty much a small bungalow that housed almost every tool that Jackson's ever made or sold – and a few that it didn't. Dad, as it turned out, had a plan.

I was 12 when I last threw a fist in anger. Patrick Wilkinson and I had a running feud at school over a rugby tackle during PE; mainly because he was the star player and I had stopped him getting a try. After about three weeks of verbal, he waited with a few mates for me in the park I used cut through to get home from school. It was only me and him fighting, the others stood and watched.

He threw the first punch, which hit my nose and made it bleed straight off. I threw one back and missed, allowing him to knee me in the stomach. I dropped to the floor, winded. Paddy's mates were shouting for him to "finish me". He strode over to do just that when I caught him with a sharp right uppercut to the bollocks. He collapsed to the floor in a heap and the fight was over. He may still be lying in the same spot now for all I know.

I became the kid who "knocked out" Paddy Wilkinson. I never had another fight in school and I was glad. Truth be told, I hated it. That feeling that I inflicted that level of pain on someone else. I'm no pacifist by any stretch of the imagination, but I'll avoid confrontation wherever I can. Except with Dad of course.

Even in my rugby days I never got into a scrap. I'd be happy to use my body and power in the game, but if it all kicked off I'd always talk my way out of it or leave it to the angrier blokes in the team.

Dad's plan, however, seemed to ignore the fact I hadn't thrown a fist for the best part of 20 years. But he had me convinced. When we got into his shed, he handed me a cup of coffee and laid it all out bare.

"Son, I think you're an idiot. I think you're stubborn. I think you love your mother very dearly. They are three things that we very much have in common. Whatever our differences, whatever you think of me, I always have and always will love your mother. I will lay down my life for that woman. Whatever has happened between us over the years gets left outside tonight. Tonight we have one objective and that is getting your mother out of that house safely, agreed?"

It was.

"I would lay down my life for her, as I said. But I've knackered myself out just getting over that fence and to here. There is no chance I can do anything in that house other than get me and your mother hurt or worse. You on the other hand..."

There was still no sign of action from the cops down on the main road. In the house we could see some movement in the main living room. The lights were off, but there were definitely people in there. A couple of bedroom lights were on upstairs. We assumed the robbers wouldn't be so stupid as to leave them on if they were in there, so that was to be my way in. But first I had to get kitted up.

Dad pulled out what looked like a set of thermal underwear – black long johns and long-sleeved turtleneck – and threw them my way. They were made of a slash-resistant, Kevlar-type material. There was a thicker vest to pull over the top and arm guards that covered my hands and forearms. The knuckles on the gloves had a metal lining to protect the wearer in case an electric saw slipped onto the hand. Well, that was how Jackson's had intended them at least. Dad's company had also created light-weight but reinforced work boots. Think steel toe-capped ballet shoes.

He grabbed a neck protector and face mask from another drawer and then gave me some headgear. It looked like a woolly hat from a distance but had the protective qualities of a crash helmet. Dad then strapped a tool belt around my waist and stashed a hammer, screwdrivers, a Jackson's knife and a few other items into it. "Are you sure you've never done this before Dad?" I asked, but he wasn't in the mood for wisecracks. He put a few more into a backpack before saying the most surprising thing of what was already a pretty messed-up evening.

"You don't look too different from Ace Stone, son."

What? How did he even know the name Ace Stone, let alone what he looked like? Then the stubborn old bastard told me.

"Being pissed off with you and thinking you're a disrespectful little shit doesn't mean I can't have some pride in you. I just don't have to tell you."

I didn't know whether to hug him or hit him. I did neither.

"Right, let's go get your mother."

The plan was for Dad to go in through the front door and put the robbers off their stride. He would just say he wanted to make sure his wife was OK and hopefully be enough of a distraction while I entered the house through the first floor bedroom. It wasn't too tricky to get up there as there was cast iron guttering and a downpipe to take my weight. Once up, there was a balcony to climb onto and the French doors wouldn't take much to open either.

We had our hopes pinned on them not giving Dad too much of a going over and then keeping him in a room separate from Mum. That would mean them splitting up. They would also, with a bit of luck, send one off to check around in case someone else was outside. That would split them further. Divide and conquer.

But what we hadn't counted on was what I was seeing now. Although the light was on, the bedroom wasn't empty. Lying on the bed and actually sleeping was one of these fuck-nuggets who'd broken in. Clearly he thought they were there for the long-haul and needed a power-nap.

I managed to open the door silently and thought taking the first one of these idiots down would be like taking sweets from a baby. But at that moment Dad began knocking at the front door and shouting, "Let me in. Let me see my wife".

Shit.

Matey-boy in the bed woke up with a start and then saw the massive ninja stood across the room frozen to the spot – aka me.

"What the fu…"

That was all he managed before I launched myself at him fists first. It was pretty dramatic. Think Superman flying and it was that sort of pose, only with a lot less grace.

My first fist skimmed across the left-hand side of his cheek and down the side of his face. At best, it roughed up his ear a little. Made it sting like when you get a ball in the face on a cold day. The other fist connected with his clavicle. That clearly inflicted more pain on him, but also in my right hand. I was sure I'd broken or dislocated something. It really fucking hurt. That's my drawing hand too. Oddly, that was all I was thinking at that precise moment. I suppose it's normal when your livelihood depends on it.

Fortunately, gravity and physics were taking care of the crook in front of me. Because having launched myself through the air, the only thing to stop me was this guy's face. I had enough comprehension of the situation to put my head down and allow the reinforced woolly hat thing I was wearing to smash his nose this way and that. He crumpled into a pile and I punched him in the face, again hurting my hand in the process.

This wasn't like the films – or my graphic novels for that matter. It's not one punch and the guy is knocked out. He was groggy, but still very much awake. And so I literally went old school and toe-punted the prick square in the bollocks.

His face took me right back to that fight with Paddy Wilkinson. The mouth is open like the person is screaming, but there is no sound coming out. While he was stunned, I quickly grabbed a pillow from the bed, pulled the pillow case off and used it to tie around his head as a gag.

The guy was lying on his front with both hands underneath encasing his throbbing nut sack. I took out a couple of plastic ties from the tool kit Dad had given me and bound his feet. Then I put my knee in the small of his back and dragged one hand and then the other around and tied them too.

He was starting to get a voice back now despite the gag. All I could think of was to grab the duvet, wrap him in it to muffle the sound and then rolled him against the bed.

One down and three to...SMASH!

learly the noise from the scuffle had alerted the other goons, one of whom was now at the door of the room and had walloped me over the head with a vase. The protective headgear did a big chunk of its job, but it still really hurt.

I suppose when you think about knights in medieval times with those big metal buckets on their heads; they're still gonna get hurt if they get whacked round the bonce with an axe.

Anyway, I was down on one knee when I saw the handle of a hammer poking out from the kit bag. I yanked it out and brought it down swiftly on my new assailant's foot. It was only after doing so that I realised it was actually a Jackson's Slappy Hammer.

Now if you're not a workman or into DIY, you may not have heard of this tool. It's like a normal hammer in much of its look, but it allows you to load the head with nails. So instead of you putting your pinkies at risk by holding the nail when you whack it, the Slappy Hammer delivers it right to the X. Then you grab your normal hammer – probably a Jackson's too – and finish the job.

But what that meant right now was that I had just put a six-inch nail through the top of this moron's Adidas, through his foot, through the sole of his trainer and then into the floorboards. And that meant he couldn't move around as well as before.

So while he screamed, I stood up with force and punched him square on the bottom of the chin with an uppercut. The skin split and sent blood gushing out. But once again a spike of pain shot through my fingers and up my forearm.

This guy was clearly more used to being in fights than me because as I stood there wincing like a girl, he composed himself and lunged for me. Well, as best he could with a foot nailed to the floor.

He grabbed hold of my hands and tried to wrestle the Slappy Hammer from my grasp. My brain was showing me the foresight of what would happen if he got it. Long story short, it would in-volve one of those nails meeting the aforementioned brain.

Distracted by my stupid head, the raider took the opportunity to head-butt my face mask. Again the Jackson's product partly did its job in protecting me, but the force of the plastic being pushed into my face was really painful and cut into my flesh.

The other guy now had the upper hand. I was losing grip on the Slappy Hammer, my head was hurting from the vase, my fingers hurt from all the punching, my face hurt from the head-butt and I was really, really knackered already. You don't see that in the films either.

I had to think and act quickly. I stamped as hard as I could on the nailed foot and as he yelped, he relinquished his grasp enough for me to try and yank the Slappy Hammer free.

But the force of pulling it free sent me into a spin, turning the full 360 and clattering the heavy tool against the wall. It fell to the ground with a thud, hitting Mum's polished sideboard on the way down and taking a chunk of wood with it.

I swiftly composed myself and got back into a fighting position, but there was no need. The guy's hands were clasped together in a praying position. And to add to the religious symbolism, there was a fucking great nail going right through the pair of them; pinning them to the wall. He passed out with the pain. Finally.

My thoughts turned to Mum and Dad. But then quickly back to this guy as he slumped in the doorway, his flesh and muscle and whatever else is in your hand tugging at the nail. Yuk. It made my skin crawl. I peeked out onto the landing to check the coast was clear, ran across and fetched a chair from one of the spare rooms and tucked it under the bloke. Hopefully that would keep him from falling.

From the window on the landing I could see out to the main road where Chief Super Whatshisname stood. There was definitely a commotion going on. More activity than earlier when I was down there, but they were still all that side of the gate.

The problem I had now was there were two men left to tackle and two parents. If I go to where Mum is, the other guy threatens Dad – or worse. And vice versa. Or if they're all in the same room it becomes a clusterfuck. Plus going down those big bastard stairs Dad had put in in the entrance hallway would leave me completely out in the open. If one of these guys does have a gun, I would be down before, well, before I was down.

I went back past old nail hands and bollock kick, through the bedroom window, down the guttering and around the back of the house. It was dark and I was able to peek through the windows to get a better idea of what was going on.

Shit. Shit. What should I do? Fuck. This was a stupid idea. Fucking terrible. We shouldn't have got involved. These guys are more likely to do something stupid now and hurt Mum or Dad. I should've waited. It's fucking Dad's fault. It was his idea to do this. And once again I'm the one left on the outside. The one left churned up emotionally. Do I go back to the cops? Fuck. I don't know what's the right thing to do.

Just then I saw Dad run across the hallway with his hands tied behind his back. He ran into the living room chased by one of the men, who tripped him from behind. Shit, I've got to get in there.

That was my first thought and I went to go in through the back door, but then I saw Dad nodding furiously towards his study as he struggled with the guy on top of him. That must be where Mum is.

Right Charlie Reid, stop feeling sorry for yourself now you sad sack. You made your choices in life. You chose to get angry. You chose not to engage. You chose everything. Now sort yourself out and get in there.

I took three very deep breaths and considered the only question I could at this point: What would Ace Stone do?

Evelyn Jackson sat in her husband's study, bound to a wooden chair by bits of the curtain that had been torn off by the scumbags who had broken into her home. One of them was directly across the hall from her now in the living room, pounding fist after fist into her husband Archie, who was flat down on his face unable to protect himself.

Her view was partially blocked by another of the raiders, who stood looking on at the assault while also glancing towards the upstairs where they had all heard bashing and crashing and that blood-curdling scream.

Goodness knows what had happened. But they knew that one of the guys who went upstairs to check on his friend hadn't returned. And the friend who went up earlier hadn't been seen again either.

Initially Evelyn thought armed police were storming the place, but when she saw it was Archie knocking at the door rather than men in armour and with guns, her heart sank a little.

She had been slapped around the face, spat at and abused. They had threatened to kill her grandson if she didn't open the safe, and so she had done. Tears ran down her face and stung a cut by her mouth. She could see the police lights on the main road, but the fact Archie was here and not them told her now that they probably wouldn't be coming.

Poor, brave Archie. He had been punched and roughed up after he came in. The intruders tore his shirt off to check he wasn't wearing a wire and issued threat after threat. They had only just started tying him up when we all heard the commotion upstairs. They all listened – the raiders, Evelyn and Archie – not knowing what to do. Then it all went quiet for about ten minutes. One of the men said he was going to check and the other disagreed.

While they argued Archie made a run for the other room and was brought down by one of the assailants. Evelyn felt sick as the man punched her husband in his side once again. Archie wasn't moving. He was a tough old boot, but these men were so much younger and stronger.

Just then the window in the study smashed through as a large figure in black flew in and landed with a roll on the floor. In a second he was back to his feet and he ran towards the door as the intruder in the way turned half in panic, half in readiness for battle.

But the man in black was too quick and too powerful. He stepped up onto the arm of a chair and launched himself feet first, spinning in the air as he drove the bottom of his two size 11s into the face of the onrushing assailant, who went crashing to the floor.

The man in black was then up again, sprinting across the hallway to intercept the thug who had been pummelling Archie. By now he was on his feet, but the rescuer had pulled a large-headed mallet from his belt and clocked the guy around the jaw and he fell to the ground in a heap unconscious.

The man in black ran to Archie and undid the binds keeping his hands behind his back. He rolled him over and helped him up.

Both turned as Evelyn let out a high-pitched shriek. The man in black looked to the floor and saw the raider he had poleaxed with a flying kick beginning to stir. He turned and sprinted back.

ad was fine. A couple of black eyes for sure, maybe damage to his ears and possibly a broken rib or two; but he would be OK. Mum looked really shaken up, but alright physically. That was the last of these bastards down and now we just had to get out of there and let the police, finally, do their job and arrest these arseholes.

But then Mum let out a scream. The bloke in the doorway a few yards from her was starting to get up. I let go of Dad and ran back across the hallway. But as I got closer I realised Mum's eyes weren't right. She wasn't looking at the man on the floor or at me or even across the hall at Dad. She was looking at the stairs. Shit. Someone was coming down the stairs.

I recognised the man as soon as I turned. It was the first guy I had taken down in the bedroom upstairs. It stood to reason I suppose. He had the longest time to recover. He had the time to get free of the ties I put round his ankles and wrists.

He was still walking gingerly after that kick to the bollocks and using one hand to lean against the wall as he came down the stairs. In his other hand was a pistol that was pointed directly at me. I turned as he fired and I felt the bullet scrape across the side of my head.

I had never felt pain like it. It was like a million migraines had been triggered all at once. I crumpled to the floor in agony. Mum shrieked, "Nooo."

She wasn't aware that the headgear I had on was protective, but the attacker had worked it out. He yanked off the face mask and the hat. Mum let out another squeal as she realised for the first time that this oversized ninja trying to rescue her was her son.

"Charlie, no," she wept as the intruder pointed the gun inches from the back of my head. I saw her wince as he began to pull the trigger. In that moment it all happened like they say it does. Christmases at the old house, learning to ride my bike, holidays in the south of France, primary school, secondary school, first kiss, first shag, first beer, first spliff, rows, drawing, university, rows, Goa, Mia, Thailand, rows, home, marriage, happiness, Oliver – God no, poor Oliver.

There was a loud thwacking sound and that was it.

The intruder collapsed to the ground with an almighty thud; the gun spilling from his hand and sliding across the tiled floor. It took me a few seconds to realise that I was still alive. The pain was still there across the back of my skull from the first shot, but there hadn't been a second.

Behind me, standing over me now with a hand on my shoulder, was my father. In his other hand was a Jackson's Slappy Hammer. I looked back at the man on the floor and could see where the six-inch nail had entered the side of his head and then where it had come out through the top. It looked like one of those joke arrows. But this was no joke. This man could be dead. Dad might've killed someone. But then he had saved me, his only son. And his wife, my beautiful mother.

Outside, a stream of police officers began sprinting up the drive-way towards the house. There were a lot more of them now and it seemed that the sound of gunfire had triggered a response.

"You need to go son, you need to get out of here." I wasn't sure why Dad was saying it at first, but he soon explained. "I can say I was protecting my property and my wife. Self-defence. Reasonable force. I don't think it'll be the same for you. You need to go."

I knew what he was saying was probably true, but I didn't want to leave Mum now. It was only when she whispered for me to go that I did. Out the window at the back of the study, around the tree, across the garden and into Dad's work shed. I quickly pulled off as much of the protective gear as I could and then put my jeans, t-shirt and hoodie over the top of the leggings and turtle-neck base layer.

I cut back through the hole in the fence and through next-door's garden. Luckily the couple who lived there had now taken an interest in what was going on, had left their house and were now standing out the front, which meant the gates were open and didn't need climbing again.

A PC standing on the opposite side of the road looked directly at me. I froze on the spot. I looked at her. I was rumbled. She knew what had happened; what I had done. I could see it in her eyes. But then she smiled and nodded and I knew that she understood.

"What's going on?" I asked Chief Superintendent Howerton as innocently as I could after finding him among the commotion.

"Mr, er, Reid, we thought, er, well, er someone has gone into the house. We thought you and your father had…You look quite rough Mr Reid, are you OK?"

"My mother is being held hostage Chief Superintendent; how should I look? And My father and I don't speak very much if you must know so I spend as little time with him as possible."

"Er, yes, someone did say. Well it seems your father has gone into the house, as did another, er, individual and the four suspects are now down. Our officers will be taking all four to hospital for checks and treatment as there are some serious injuries inflicted upon them. We expect three of them to be in custody later this morning, while the fourth has a serious head wound that may require more treatment."

"My Dad did all that?"

"It is too soon to say that. We believe another individual entered the house at around the same time as your father. But it seems your father certainly had a role in bringing this situation to its conclusion. Where have you been Mr Reid?"

"I was waiting over there with your PC." The officer again nodded in response. I was clear.

Mum and Dad both recovered from their physical injuries. Mum took longer to get over the psychological ones and needed some help. We had them both stay at our house over Christmas. It was cramped but we managed.

One of the news agencies gathered at the front of Mum and Dad's that morning had managed to get pictures of a masked man in black in the upstairs bedroom window and another of him running across the driveway towards the outbuildings.

The police had issued them to the media in an attempt to trace the individual. A spokesman decried vigilantism. The comments on Facebook and other sites were more complimentary.

The cops spoke to me a few times, trying to get me to admit I had been there. Why else would my right hand be in a cast and I have a black eye? I denied it and had three alibis – Pavel the driver, the smiling PC and Chief Superintendent Howerton. If I wasn't with one, I was with the other, clearly.

They asked Dad if it was me in the house too. He told them: "Charlie? My son Charlie? Are you joking? That wet blanket is as useless as a chocolate teapot. He might draw superheroes in comics, but that's where it begins and ends. He's a fucking waste of space." I think he enjoyed acting up the part. At least I hope he was acting.

Oliver saw the news footage and the photo of the man in black.

"He looks so cool Dad. It looks like he's got a robot face and awesome weapons. You should draw him Daddy and do a story about him."

Then later that night, as I tucked him in bed and he snuggled with the new Thor cuddly toy Nan and Grandad got, he asked: "So does this now mean that superheroes are real?"

"Maybe son, maybe."

HIGH NOON

I was lying on the sofa reading a book when he appeared out of nowhere. He just ran across the wooden floor in the lounge at a great rate of knots. But then he stopped dead in his tracks, turned and looked up at me.

Of course, I froze on the spot. This was quite a big spider and I could tell that this one was out to kill me. I must have chucked his mother out of the bedroom window when I was a kid or stamped on his dad during my teens. I wasn't sure which exactly, but it was clear vengeance was on his mind today.

He remained dead still on the same spot for a couple of minutes. But, to be honest, so had I. There was no chance of me moving yet. At least the panic breathing hadn't kicked in.

I could feel each of his very many eyes piercing towards me. My mind drifted to the film Arachnophobia. I needed to get my hands on one of those nail guns so I could just sit safely on the sofa, feet off the ground, and shoot the bastard from here.

My day-dream lasted for only a few seconds because when I came back to the real world, the hairy little bastard had moved. My whole body began to tingle. Then I felt a tickle on my cheek.

'Had the spider leapt onto me and was now crawling up onto my face?' I wondered. No. Some of my long, dark hair has slipped round onto my face. Phew. I knew it was my hair all along.

I spotted the spider over by the fireplace. He had taken up the same stance as earlier and stared at me, almost as if he was a statue that had been moved to a new placement in the room.

Now, this visit from the spider was at rather an inopportune moment as I was trying to watch the second part of a drama on the telly. Amazingly, having watched the first part the night before, I found myself at home, with nothing to do when the next part was broadcast. Imagine that! In the days of watch-when-you-want telly and box sets.

But I couldn't take my eye off the spider to watch the telly in case he disappeared. If that happened and I couldn't find him again, I wouldn't be able to sleep tonight. He would surely find me and crawl all over my face, in my mouth and ears, up my nose. Maybe he's a she and she might lay her eggs in some orifice! That could not happen.

I swallowed an imaginary bravery pill and stood up. He moved, I shit myself and jumped back on the sofa. Damn you. But I still had to get rid of him. The old glass and paper routine would be called upon once again.

I walked backwards to the kitchen because I didn't want to let him out of my sight. I returned slowly with the glass and the paper to find the spider in the same position. I could see him laughing at me for being such a big wuss.

"I'll get you, you smug little prick." I couldn't believe I was talking to a spider. But it make me feel like the hero in the final scene of an action movie as he confronts the bad guy and stops his plot to rule the world, "Mwoa ha ha ha!"

The spider continued to laugh at me as about ten times on the trot I reached forward to put the glass over it only to swiftly recoil in fear, despite him not even moving. Like a really bad effort at slapsies.

This was going to take tremendous courage from me to overcome this source of all evil. I took a step back and stood tall.

"Hiiin the blue corner, standing at over six feet tall and weighing in at 14 stone, the challenger, Paul 'The Hunter' Carter." Crowd cheers.

"And in the living room corner, standing at about one inch tall, and weighing in at not much really, the House Spider." Boo, boo, booo.

Again I realised I was on my own talking to a spider and felt slightly embarrassed. I turned my thoughts back to the eight-legged critter.

"Right you little shit. You come into my house, stroll round like you own the place, stop me from watching my programme with that bloke who used to be in some soap opera that I didn't watch. Well I'm not standing for it anymore."

Bang. Well it was more of a dumph really, or was it a clink? Doesn't matter really, all you need to know is that I had put the glass on top of the spider and he was now trapped. "Haha! Victory!"

I slipped the piece of paper under the cup with ease. But despite his position, the spider was still in control. I could see him scuttling around in the glass, like an angry lion just before feeding time.

I now had to lift the cup and paper in a well-timed, well-positioned manner, in order to remove this intruder from the house. If I got it wrong, he would be free again in an instant.

And that piece of paper is only, well, paper thin. I would, in effect, be touching him and his fat, black, hairy legs. Euuck. That made my skin crawl.

My attention was taken by the TV, on which my drama had gone into the first ad break. I had missed the first 20 minutes and – as I found out later – two more people had died. One was that comedian who thought he'd have a go at straight acting and the other one was the guy I thought was the killer.

"Bloody right, no more nonsense."

I walked over to my captive and laughed. I was going to rid my life of this, this, this creature forever.

I pressed firmly down on the top of the cup, and carefully slid my hand under the paper. It took about eight minutes on and off.

I could feel and see the spider going ape-shit. He knew his time was up. He knew the challenger had won. He knew his reign was over.

Speaking of reign, I felt the rain-soaked concrete dampen my socks as I jogged down the road holding the glass/spider/paper combination.

Obviously I didn't want to just chuck him outside my house, because he would find a way back in pretty sharpish.

Two roads down, I thought I had reached a safe distance – now to let him free. How the hell do I do that?

It was a serious quandary. If I lift the glass, he'll be there on the paper ready to leap at me. And if I pull the paper away, he'll fall straight down on the floor and climb up my trouser leg.

I was already at full pace when I heard the glass land on the back patio of 43 Gosling Street having flung the glass/spider/paper combo over their fence. By the time they got outside to see what had happened, I would be back home. Aaaand with their back door now open while they checked, the spider would run in and take up residence in their house – if he/she/it was still alive.

My other half was pulling on to the driveway as I arrived back at our front door. "Where have you been in your pyjamas?" she asked.

"Oh, there was a big spider running through the lounge, so I thought I'd get chuck him out sharpish before you got home love. I know you don't like them."

Well, it was mostly true.

BEASTS AND BUSINESS

ight, that's it for tonight fuckers. I'm drained. And I need to wank while I still have the energy. Any questions, stick them in the comments in the Facebook thread and I will answer them tomorrow. And Niall? Stay. Away. From. Dogs. Goodnight."

Daniel Merriwinkle lifted the huge skull-shaped glass from his desk and downed the remainder of the generous helping of Grey Goose vodka in one. He clicked the mouse to end the session, turned off his MacBook and chuckled to himself. He had just spent the last 90 minutes hosting a webinar in his business coaching group and it had been a lot of fun. And he got paid for this shit. He grabbed his phone and messaged his mentor, Maximilian Alfonse.

"Another great session Max, did you hear?"

"Yep. Well done Dan. You should be proud of yourself. You've really come a long way."

"Jesus Max, you sound like a fucking X Factor judge." But he was right – he was always right – it had been quite a journey for Dan. Fuck it, it had been a journey for Max too as he dragged this frankly fucked-up individual from the gutter by the lapels, and coached and tutored him towards the promised land of financial freedom. His disciple was currently the head of a thriving coaching community – one that had multiple spin-off businesses bringing in the megabucks he had dreamed of as a boy.

He used to worry about buying a sandwich from Pret as it was too expensive. But now he could buy a Rolex, a new Audi, a villa in Thailand or a dozen prostitutes and a shit-load of top-quality cocaine without a second thought as to the cost. He was a real life entrepreneur now with more fingers in more pies than he'd had hot dinners – not all of them entirely kosher, but he kept those to himself. Max knew, of course. He knew everything about Dan. It was his job to.

Three years earlier, the outlook was very different. In fact, it literally looked like a huge pile of shit. Dan stood at the door of a tiny toilet cubicle staring at it in disbelief. There was no Max at that point. No expensive vodka glugged from crystal skulls. Not much of anything of any real value.

The toilet bowl was filled to tipping point with brown, sludgy excrement. The stench was so horrific that it had already triggered a headache of epic proportions and Dan's eyes were red and streaming. It may just have been tears, it was hard to tell.

But that scenario left him contemplating one very serious question.

Actually, scrub that, there were two – the second of which was how in the holy world of fuck could such a pristine group of females that made up the dance troupe at Delights strip club conjure up such a putrid, gag-inducing pile of faeces from their arseholes?

For example, stood next to Dan right now was Cheryl – a performing name that was given due to her very vague likeness to the former Girls Aloud singer. That said, she was strikingly beautiful; a delicate flower who needed little if any make-up and whose smile had men melting in the palm of her hand. And when she spoke? Wow. Her soft, sensual tones had them pulling twenties and fifties out of their wallets before she'd even taken off an item of clothing. Then there was her incredible body. She was no more than 5ft 5ins tall and without a glimmer of fat, and punters – male and female alike – found her breasts mesmeric.

She was of a class way above this place that was for sure. And so the idea that she could produce anything that contributed to the swamp of poo that lay before them was just mind boggling.

Just then, a gurgle rippled up through the system. As a big bubble burst through the top layer on the bog, it pushed a small wave of shit over the sides of the bowl and down towards the floor. At the same time, a mirror reaction triggered in Cheryl.

Dan watched her put one hand to her stomach as it twinged and baulked, then the other hand flew up to her mouth in a feeble attempt to block what was coming. Two seconds later the burrito and two glasses of wine she had downed at lunch spewed out from her gullet and onto the floor, mixing into the streams of shit to form the unholiest of cocktails.

All of which brings us to that first – and more profound – question Dan had been contemplating: "How the fuck did I get here?"

It was a valid question. Six months earlier he had been working in the City on a six-figure salary, plus bonuses, plus perks, plus pension, plus share options. He had been the rising star of a high-end recruitment firm – and had just delivered what was potentially the company's biggest ever contract after months and months of persistence and charm.

Dan had found the person in charge of recruitment at a major aerospace company. He sent her an expensive bottle of champagne and a basket of fresh fruit as a warm up. Then he rang to offer his services as the talented head-hunter he was to fill any vacancies she had with the best candidates. She told him she wasn't interested.

"No problem, I understand," Dan replied. "I'll ring you next Tuesday at 11 just to see if anything has changed."

He rang her again exactly when he said he would. But the answer on the second week was still no. And the third. The fourth came with the additional "…and I can categorically say we will never hire through you so you can stop calling". He didn't. The weekly calls got less frosty, but the answer was still always no. The breakthrough came in week 14 when Dan didn't call – and she called him to check everything was OK. But the answer was still no.

Over the next few weeks, Mrs Challinor became Susan, then Sue and then Suzi-Sue. They talked about her love of golf (which Dan hated), her daughter's horse and her ex-husband's midlife crisis that saw him secretly remortgage their house to buy a Ferrari that he hid from her and used at weekends to pull impressionable young (and as the court heard, sometimes underage) women at a nightclub in the City.

But still the answer to Dan's offer was no. Until week 24.

Although their calls were strictly 11am on a Tuesday, Suzi-Sue called at 9.20am on a Monday. She had been let down and needed a position filled quickly or she was in the shit.

She gave Dan the opportunity.

"If I do this, you have to promise that you'll put all your recruitment work our way from now on," Dan told her.

"You wan….I can't put all of it your way, but I will some."

"I think I'm busy today, I'm not sure I can help."

"Dan, I simply can't do that beca…."

"Sorry, I think I have a call coming through on the other line."

"Alright, alright. You blackmailing prick. You've got it – but only if you deliver this time." Dan loved it when she put on her stern voice and told her so with a big grin on his face.

He had the position filled before lunch; a prime candidate perfectly suited to the role and available to start at once. Boom. That afternoon came the contract offer for the company to handle all the recruitment. It would be worth a lot of money to the firm and Dan in the months ahead.

Dan was dry-humping the edge of his desk and circling an imaginary lasso above his head in celebration when the company's CEO Chris McDonald politely tapped on the door of his office. He did not look so chipper, certainly not in a rodeo mood.

He explained there had been meetings, profits were down, costs had gone up, there had to be restructuring, some departments would merge, others would close, but in short, Dan's services were no longer required. The mega-deal he had just landed made no difference – "Thank you of course Dan, it will be a great source of income going forward" – but the decision had been made and was final.

The irony of being a recruitment specialist and unable to find himself a job in his chosen field was not lost on Dan. It was like he had been black-balled. Maybe it was because he hated golf. Maybe it was because he had called his boss a talentless, coke-sniffing, cockwomble. Who knows? In truth, his heart wasn't really in it anyway. It was never his calling in life, just a job – albeit a very well paid one.

However, bills still needed to be paid. Having decided to stay in London while he tried to find work, Dan soon found himself living on the breadline. His accommodation got smaller and emptier. And the choice between dinner and paying for a Travelcard to get to the next job interview was a regular occurrence.

He started out working at a gym and when the offer of some doorman work at the strip club came along, he took it. Dan was, after all, a well-built lump of a man with a thick beard, stern glare and quick wit suited to being a bouncer. There was, though, the bonus of hanging around with gorgeous, half-naked women all day.

He also took on some additional odd-job work at the club to add a few extra pennies to the weekly take-home. But he had not been prepared for the cauldron of sloppy, bubbling shit that now stood before him. And one other thing had since become abundantly clear. The yellow Marigold gloves he had put on to protect himself from the turgid excrement only came halfway up his hefty forearm and to unblock this loo he was going to have to go at least elbow-deep.

For fuck's sake.

A buzz on the intercom slowly snapped Dan out of the memory of the strip club shit-fest, past his first encounter with Max – a critical meeting that set him on the path to becoming first a personal trainer, then a gym owner, a copywriter, a marketing expert, social media wunderkind and a business coaching guru with cash to burn – and back to the present.

Dan necked another gulp of Grey Goose and answered the call.

"Hey Dan, it's Tenk. Let me in buddy."

Tenk was Dan's friend and consigliere in his business. A brilliant number two and a tech and video genius who proved to be another vital cog in achieving the success he had so far. He was lively and full of smiles. The pair usually worked from their respective home offices, but Tenk had come to Dan's pad in Brighton tonight as they had a business planning weekend ahead.

They would spend a few hours on work, then head out to the arcades and buy shit from the shops on the seafront. After lunch they would spend a few more hours on the business before going to a spa to pretty themselves up ahead of a night on the town. With a bit of luck, they would both bring a girl or two back to the apartment. A double-team was not unheard of. A sniff and a gulp on the Sunday morning and they would be ready to repeat the work/fun cycle again. But that was tomorrow.

Dan showed Tenk to the guest room, although he'd stayed here a dozen times before, and then poured him a drink while helping himself to another skull-full of vodka.

An hour or so later, they had already started their planning to the soundtrack of cheesy 80s pop hits and were well on the way to world domination. They were working in an industry that was growing exponentially month by month and they decided they needed to do something big and soon to give them a leg-up to making their real fortune. And the fortune was there to be made.

Dan told Max that he wanted to speak at a top event on the same stage as one of the industry's major players. Standing on the shoulders of giants and all that. And as Dan and Tenk sank their drinks, refilled and then drank some more, they decided that they would put on their own event. A huge event in a big arena packed with wannabe entrepreneurs desperate to learn how to be the next big thing.

They would book a huge name to headline. A Branson, a Robbins, a Zuckerberg, a Vaynerchuk, a Musk, a Gates, a Cusick – someone who wouldn't be cheap, but would sell the place out no problems. And Dan would be the warm-up man, as it were.

It would propel him to super-stardom in the world of business speaking. He would give himself equal billing and he would steal the show on the night with his charisma and charm. The crowd would be eating out of his hand and the door to Club Multi-Millionaire would be opened for him by big-boobed girls in gold bikinis. He would be on his way, with Tenk loyally at his side also reaping the benefits. They drank a toast or two or three and the night ended in a haze and alcohol and laughter.

Dan stood proudly with his legs astride and his hands on his hips. A small breeze ruffled the thick black hair on his back and arse cheeks. He was completely naked. But he worried not, for his body right now was in awesome shape. His quads were the size of an average man's waist, his torso trim and toned, pecs flexing like a house party was going off inside, and his guns could lift a bus. And not an empty bus – oh no – but one filled with day-trippers on a tour around London. But he could not see the sights of London now, nor Brighton for that matter. It was all white. Clouds. He was in the clouds. He took a step forward and the pillow below cushioned his foot. He looked around and saw mile upon mile ahead with the most beautiful rainbow at the end. And there was someone there, near the foot of the rainbow, but it was too far for him to make out. But he knew he wanted to be near that mystery individual. Dan put his fingers to his mouth to whistle, but all that came out was raspberry and a bit of dribble. He never could quite get the hang of that. Puzzled for a second, he retook his stance and shouted, "Oi, over here." This wasn't to the distant figure; that person was far too far away. Instead, by his side now was the most glorious black unicorn your mind could ever consider. This beautiful creature – with fine mane of hair, and an enormous, resplendent horn jutted out in front – would help carry Dan to his promised land. Dan leapt onto its back, being careful not to crush his cock and balls in the process, and gave the command, "Tenk, to the rainbow." Tenk began to trot at first but was soon at a full, light-speed gallop across the plains of cloud and towards the foot of the rainbow. As they got ever-closer, Dan tried to make out the figure in the distance. It was clear they also had their own unicorn, a white one. The figure sat side-saddle and had huge breasts – that was something he could see. But the face was still a blur. Then a noise arose from around him. It sounded like flutes, harps maybe, and cymbals being tapped lightly. Dan couldn't focus. The rainbow and the clouds began to fade, as did the unicorn and the figure in the distance. But oddly, the face began to come into focus. It did not match the perfect figure of a woman with the massive norks. It didn't even look real. Dan shook his head and looked again. It was a drawing. A sketch of a man. He had a huge fat face with bulging eyes and glasses. And a crazily big grin. And an enormous nose. The noise around Dan became more familiar now. It wasn't music; it was the annoying boing and shrills of his phone notifications. And the face was as clear as day now. It was Maximilian Alfonse. Max was ringing him right now.

Dan woke up.

Dan first met Maximilian Alfonse when he was working at the strip club. It was on the night of the toilet shit-fest in fact. He had been clearing up and checking the booths when he spotted a man asleep in one of them.

"Time to go home mate, we're closed," Dan had said.

"I'll pay you to let me stay here," came the mumbled reply, the guy's face buried into the beautifully upholstered but stained seating.

"Where do you live mate? We'll get you a cab."

"Utah."

"Ah. Well where's your hotel?"

"I don't have one. Just let me stay here. I won't cause any trouble."

That was more than Dan's job was worth and he needed it right now. Plus those toilets still weren't to be trusted.

Dan thought about just carrying the bloke out and leaving him in the gutter, but he was too kind-hearted for that. He ended up carrying him back to his apartment and fixing him a sandwich. The guy, Max, had perked up a bit by now and they stayed up till daylight chatting about life and business while necking lots of vodka.

Max, as he had mentioned, was American. He was very successful. He told Dan he was a multi-millionaire entrepreneur with business interests across the globe. He was in the UK to meet with some associates about a new project. Another venture that would be a huge success. The meeting ended with several thousand pounds spent on booze, cocaine, MDMA and strippers.

This was normal life for Max though, so he had a lot more staying power than most. Everyone else had left or was carried out by their chauffeur by the time he eventually hit his limit and passed out. It was nearly 4am when he and Dan collided.

For Dan, it was a turning point in his life. Max was only about five or six years older, but he seemed to have everything Dan wanted. Where do you see yourself in five years' time? With a string of successful businesses, a load of money in the bank, and a big Rolex and hot-as-balls girlfriend on my arm, Dan told his new friend. "I'll drink to that."

Max had gone by the time Dan woke the next morning. But there was a note left under his mobile: "Thanks for your hospitality Dan. I won't forget it. Great chatting to you. You've got real potential. I've added my number on your phone. Message me anytime if you need anything, ever. Max."

Underneath his name was a little drawing of a man with a huge fat face, bulging eyes, glasses, a crazily big grin and an enormous nose.

Dan took a picture of the avatar and used it as Max's contact image on his phone. It was the same drawing Dan had seen atop that fine female body in his dream. He thought about it for a moment and then quickly shook it loose.

Dan decided to speak to Max now and picked up the phone. He told him about the messed up dream, but didn't mention the nakedness or tits. That was a bit too weird.

And he told him about the plan he and Tenk had come up with.

"So he'll be the headline speaker, but I'll be so on-point everyone will remember me."

"And you'll get equal billing on the promotional material."

"Exactly."

"It's going to be huge."

"Absolutely massive."

"This'll take things to the next level for sure."

"Beyond that. Stratospheric."

"Yeah man, Club Multi-Millionaire."

"There's someone at the door."

"At the door?"

"Yeah, it must be Tenk."

"Speak later."

"Bye."

"Bye."

Tenk had been listening to the conversation from the landing, but having been rumbled he gently tapped on the door.

"Come in."

Dan was sat up in a vast double bed with golden sheets and a roaring tiger embroidered on the headboard. To one side of the bed was a golden lampstand with a figurine of a naked woman holding up the bulb. One the other was an empty bottle of vodka and some lube.

Tenk wasn't sure where to look as the huge half-naked fur-ball in front of him wasn't much of a better option.

"Max loves the idea of the event Tenk, it's a go." Dan always had to get permission from his mentor before he went ahead and did something like this.

"Great, but have you seen this?" Tenk held out his smartphone displaying an advert for Chad Kilgore's X-treme Mastermind.

The X-treme Mastermind was a get-together for entrepreneurs out in the sticks in Texas where they did real yee-haw stuff like shoot guns, blow shit up, ride horses, fight, drink beer, take drugs and fuck their own cousins. And it cost $10,000 to attend the week just for the privilege of being in everyone else's company.

Dan wasn't too opposed to any of that. He'd been to loads of big-ticket masterminds in the past. And he actually thought one of his cousins was really fit, but hadn't seen much of her since he told her so. No, Dan's problem was that it was run by Chad Kilgore, who he thought was a massive prick. Brash, uncultured, unprincipled and only out for himself. Tenk thought Dan hated him so much because they were so alike, but never said so out loud.

However, there was a line in the advert that had left Dan happy to set aside their differences for now, shell out the 10k and get stateside. It read: "Mystery Guest: After a decade in isolation, the Island legend returns."

"It can't be. Gary Tremendous? Really?"

Gary Tremendous was *the* number one life coach, business guru and motivational speaker on the planet. He could command any fee he wanted just for spouting five minutes of his knowledge on stage. His books became best-sellers before they were written. Presidents and Prime Ministers had clamoured for his advice on all sorts of matters. Global corporations offered him billions to come and work for them.

And then one day, he just packed it all in and fucked off to his private island.

There were rumours he had gone primal; become disgusted with the trappings of his wealth and shed it all and lived off the land in a mud hut. Others claimed he was developing a new global communications system that would rival the internet itself. And others claimed he had killed a hooker in a hotel room and fled. The truth was no one really knew as he hadn't made any public appearance or statement in all those intervening years.

But somehow, that fuck-knuckle Chad Kilgore had not only managed to track him down but to lure him back to the States for his shitty little mastermind.

"He must've paid him a hoooooooooge amount," said Tenk.

"Yeah, that or he's got pictures of him with the dead prozzie," chipped Dan. "You know what? We've got to go. We've got to go to Texas, to the mastermind. I'm the best motherfucking salesman on this planet. Two minutes with me and I'll have him signed and sealed ready to be the headline speaker at our event. Gary Tremendous makes his London debut alongside Daniel Merriwinkle. Fucking gold."

Tenk the unicorn galloped through a lush green meadow at speed with Dan on his back. There were ancient trees around them and the sky was a brilliant blue. Dan could see a small rainbow atop the one cloud in the sky. But this was very different from the last time he rode his trusted steed. For ahead of him were rows and rows of people and he could see their faces. They were ex-girlfriends, old bosses, cruel teachers, bullies, trolls, people who had held him back or told him he would amount to nothing. People who hated him and who he loathed back. Dan looked down at his naked body and then in an instant it was covered with ornate gold armour. His now gauntlet-clad hand held in it glorious sword. He was no longer atop Tenk; instead he ran alongside his loyal companion, whose long horn glinted in the sunshine. On the other side now was Max, also in armour and carrying a huge battle-axe. They met the waiting rabble in a crash of metal, bones and blood. Dan cut and slashed, chopping down all those who stood in his way. Max obliterated bodies with a single smash, while Tenk speared others with his horn and tossed them into a void of nothingness. They were no more. Die! Die! I will conquer all. Raaahhhh! Urrrghhh! Muuurgghhh!

"Easy on the groaning there matey, you can't have a wet dream while I'm trying to eat my breakfast." The voice echoed through the sky as the last enemy fell. The voice was clear. It was not from this realm. It was from the other place. And it was Northern.

Dan woke up.

It had been four days since Dan and Tenk had found out about Gary Tremendous's appearance at the X-treme Mastermind. In that time they had booked their places, bought their plane tickets and were now coming into land at San Antonio international airport in Texas.

It had been something of an eventful flight. Dan was a nervous flier and had chosen to medicate with vodka and cocaine, which meant there were a few gaps in his recollection of the 14-hour, 5,000-mile journey time that included catching a connecting flight from Atlanta. But Tenk was on hand to fill them in.

It seems Dan had passed out at Heathrow and had to be carried on board the jet by his pal, only to wake and upset the cabin crew by yelling, "Oi big tits, get me a Goose." They declined and instead he drank from the bottle stashed in his hand luggage.

He then decided to watch a film, but somehow found something deeply emotional in the subtext of Die Hard and wept uncontrollably for 45 minutes before ripping the sleeves off his t-shirt so he could have a vest like John McClane.

Then, after repeatedly shouting, "Yippee ki yay, motherfucker" at a small child sat in front of him, he passed out again. At Atlanta he carjacked a transporter used to shuttle disabled people around the airport and crashed it, but managed to pin the blame on an elderly man who was looking for his wife.

The booze and coke caught up with him on the flight to Texas and he puked between the headrests of the seats in front, splattering a suited businessman and his done-up-to-the-nines companion in a lumpy vom rainbow. He then fell fast asleep and dreamt of unicorns and bloody battles until Tenk woke him.

Just over an hour later they had turned off Interstate 35 in the small town of Devine and were heading up a dusty backroad towards the remote ranch hosting Chad Kilgore's mastermind.

"Small City. Big Heart. Bright Future," read the town sign.

"Fucking redneck cowboy hillbillies," muttered Dan.

They arrived just before 6pm and were shown to their cabin. Although he would never say it out loud, Dan was impressed.

The wooden chalet was modern; with air con, wifi and USB points for those wishing to work. The views outside were across a vast blue lake with a beautiful forest beyond. It was no Brighton, but it would very much do for now.

Settled and changed, Dan and Tenk headed for the welcome drinks keen to find out where Gary Tremendous was and how he came to be here. But no one seemed to know anything.

Dan necked cocktail after cocktail as he mingled and chatted. And drank more and more as he came away from the conversations empty-handed.

Tenk was on the other side of the room beginning to work his charm on a girl from California who "really digs" his Doncaster accent when an almighty smash silenced the room.

Dan had drunkenly fallen onto a bar, his elbow coming down on the edge of a cocktail-laden tray, which then catapulted a few feet across the room and onto the lap of a guy who now looked seriously pissed off.

He stood and walked over to where Dan lay and looked down on him. The guy was a handsome, strapping dude with a lengthy beard covering his face and a black baseball cap turned backwards. It was Chad Kilgore.

"What the hell man?"

"Sorry, arrghh, sorry, I slipped."

"Shit. I should've known it would be you Daniel Merri-fuck. Looks like you slipped a few too many cocktails down your neck brother. You need to ease up a bit."

"Yeah?" said Dan struggling to find a footing as the alcohol, drugs and tiredness took hold. "Well you need to fuck off a bit."

Dan didn't see the fist or Tenk's attempt to stop it. He was knocked out cold.

The bodies of those Dan and his comrades had slaughtered dissolved into the ground and flowers began to bloom from the same spot. Dan removed his armour and tossed it to the ground he turned to his left and smiled at the 2D face of Maximilian Alfonse and then to his right where Tenk the black unicorn had retaken his human form. Tenk had been Dan's right-hand man as he built his business empire and it was fitting that he be here now for the moment of glory. The three men formed the points of a triangle and then put one hand atop another's before lifted them slowly to the sky. A beam of light shone down from the sun and on to Dan. Tenk and Max stepped away and slowly disappeared as Dan gathered the light in his broad chest. He could feel his power ris-

ing. He could feel his knowledge deepening. He would rule this world – starting with his EVENT! Blam. Dan pointed and directed a beam of light towards a corner of the meadow where a huge stage now emerged from the ground. As he turned in a circle, bolts of light fired from his fingertips and created huge banners bearing his name, a huge bar stacked with Grey Goose vodka served in skull glasses, there was a parade of the most stunning women you had ever seen all wearing 'I ♥ Dan' t-shirts, while the men in the audience nodded their appreciation towards the big bearded beast who proudly stood surveying all he had built. They thumped their chests, pointed at Dan and told him he was 'the man'. Dan blasted his fingers again and there was a band playing. Take That. No, no. That wasn't right. Blast! Steps? No. Come on. Where is this shit coming from? I need something more powerful. Blast. Yeah, that's it. The Prodigy. Boom. Blast again. Another shot of light and this time all the men in the audience had disappeared. Blast! The next shot of light rid all the women of their clothes. Blast! Now their morals had gone. Blast! Now all of Dan's clothes had fallen off. Blast! All of a sudden a thousand naked women walked towards him. Another blast from his fingers and they started to orgasm. And another blast from his finger. Another finger blast. Finger blast. Finger Blast. Blast. Blast. Blast. Blast. NNngggghhhh.

Dan woke up. In a mess.

After clearing up his sticky start to the day and having breakfast, Dan joined Tenk in heading out to the far reaches of the ranch to have a go at firing machine guns. They only had access to the arcade versions back on Brighton seafront, but these were the real McCoy. A Colt AR-15 loaded with real bullets. Dan was giddy with excitement.

They walked down to the range and could see where a selection of targets had been set up with huge mud banks behind them. The whole place was incredibly noisy as over on the far right of the area was another group flinging around a makeshift track in mud-buggies. Plus machine guns aren't the quietest of things either.

Tenk went first and nearly matched the gun with giggles in terms of sound. After every blast of bullets, he stopped to laugh. "This is fucking insane." He wasn't too bad a shot either, destroying a target shaped like a pig and blowing the head of the traditional 'man-shaped' one.

Then he made way for Dan, who shook the instructor's hand and listened intently to the safety instructions. "Yep, no problem." He picked up the weapon and his mind flashed back to the dream. Perhaps one of these would be better than that great big sword. Then he thought about how the last dream ended and shook his attention back to the moment.

"Right big man," said the instructor. A broad-set military man in camo gear and wraparound shades. "Stand here and give it one short blast so you get a feel of the kick back."

Dan pulled the trigger and hit the man-target right in the chest.

"Nice shot," the instructor chimed. "Now I will step back and after my five count you can fire, OK?"

"OK."

"Five...four...three...two...one...fire."

Dan gripped the handle tight in his right hand, feeling the cold metal press to his skin. The butt of the gun was pulled tight into his shoulder and he lined up the sight as he pulled again on the trigger.

The first few seconds were fine, but then the kick-back triggered a spasm in Dan's back – a hangover from his earlier years spent powerlifting. He screamed in agony and let go of the barrel of the gun with his left hand. But the right was still on the handle, still pulling the trigger and still firing as it began to pan right, right, right, right.

Chad Kilgore loved machine guns and he loved driving his mini-monster truck around mud tracks. It had been a hard choice that afternoon, but he had guns at home and not a track like this. He stamped on the accelerator of his matte black vehicle. 'Smooth as fuck,' he thought. He went up one bank, caught some air at the top and landed with a bounce that tested the suspension.

As he came down the other side of the bank, he noticed something in the dirt ahead. It looked as though someone was throwing stones into the ground with orange dust flying up with the impact; each one going closer and closer to his truck. Chad recognised the pattern almost immediately, opened the door and dived from the moving vehicle.

Back at the gun range, the instructor was in full Army mode, yelling: "Cease fire! Cease fire!" But Dan's hand was gripped tight on the trigger due to the pain in his back. It was an involuntary clench, but the gun was still firing bullet after bullet now in the direction of the off-road track where a black jeep had just landed off a jump. In the distance, Dan could just make out what looked like a figure jumping from the truck and into the dirt.

Chad landed with a thud and a roll. He got to his feet swiftly, sprinted ten yards and dived to the ground again, just as a hail of bullets tore through the front of his beloved truck, into the engine and BOOM, the whole machine burst into a ball of flames.

The explosion took the vehicle into the air and it crashed back down to earth on its roof. Fortunately, the bullets had now ceased and a quick scan around showed that other than the truck, there had been no damage to anyone or anything.

Chad stood, trying to fathom what had happened and in the distance made out the figure of Tenk jogging towards him with his palms raised in a placating manner as he shouted: "It were an accident. It were an accident."

But beyond Tenk, Chad could see the hulking figure of Dan Merriwinkle scurrying away from the range. Chad looked down at his scuffed clothes, his bleeding knees and elbows, and his wrecked truck and muttered only one word: "Motherfucker."

Dan looked out the window of his cabin and saw Chad Kilgore striding towards him flanked by two men with arms the size of juggernauts. He rightly assumed they weren't coming to ask for tips on boosting their social media profiles and went to the door to try to head off the charge.

"Chad, I…" Thwack. He hadn't got two words out of his mouth before the raging American punched him in the face.

"Pack your bags and get the fuck out of here, now." It was an appropriate enough demand, but Dan was desperate and pleaded his case.

"Look, Chad, I know what it looks like. But my back went. You can't think I tried to shoot you, do you? I'm not that good an aim."

Chad looked on unimpressed, his muscle-bound chaperones even less so.

"I will go, I promise, in the morning. I just neeeed to see Gary Tremendous speak. I just need that. Please?"

Chad's face contorted in slight puzzlement, before a grin formed across his face.

"You actually think Gary Tremendous is speaking here?"

"Well I did...your ad. It said, 'The island legend returns after ten years in isolation'."

"Hmm, yeah. An error. It was meant to say 'Ireland legend'. Typo at the agency, what can you do? It's a guy called Declan Hanratty from Dublin. Did ten years inside for armed rob…" Thwack.

This time it was Dan's turn to land a punch, although it was slightly miscued and hurt a lot more than he thought it would. He only got the one in before the security duo pounced and dragged him away towards the exit as he spewed bile in Kilgore's direction.

"You dirty, sneaky, cousin-fucking, no-morals prick…" Water off a duck's back.

an held his head under the hot shower and did all he could to hold back the tears. He was shacked up in a grotty little motel about five miles from the ranch he had been kicked out of having spent the best part of $25,000 on a fraud of an event and now faced paying out the same again to a brash wanker he absolutely hated for blowing up his truck.

At least he could enjoy a wry smile about that. But to top it all off, his so-called loyal number two Tenk had left him here alone because "technically he hadn't been kicked out" and the Californian chick was sliding some very un-mixed messages to his DMs.

"What the fuck do you do now Merriwinkle?" he asked himself in the mirror.

He was still in his bathrobe brushing his hair when there was a knock at the door. It wouldn't be room service in this place, that was for sure. He looked through the spyhole, but couldn't see anyone. A pang of fear shot through his body as he pictured himself opening the door to find and angry Chad Kilgore or one of his goons in front of him with an automatic rifle.

Another knock. But still he couldn't see anyone.

"Er, who is it? I'm, er, not dressed, I can't open the door."

"It's an old friend come to visit."

Dan recognised the voice immediately and a big grin tore across his face quicker than the bullets hit Kilgore's truck. He yanked the chain off and opened the door.

"Max!"

"And I've brought friends."

Tenk had chosen the Pine View Motel because it looked small, quaint and tidy, and not too much else around; just a grocery store and gas station across the road.

But as he came to collect his boss the next morning, he drove past twice hoping to god that this wasn't the place. The car park area was littered with sleeping bodies, empty booze bottles and all sorts of detritus. One car was overturned, several motorbikes on their sides and the swimming pool had been drained and was now housing a still-raging fire.

He went to the room that Dan had been staying in. The glass in the window had been shattered and the curtains were now flapping on the outside. The brown door was also broken and only clinging to the frame by a couple of screws on the bottom hinge. Spilling out of the door on the floor was a trail of bed sheets and Grey Goose bottles. Inside the room lay several half-naked women, more vodka bottles, a pile of white powder, lube and used condoms. But no Dan.

A caretaker appeared at Tenk's side. The man had a face full of wrinkles that told him he had seen some things in his days. Perhaps not like this though. Who knows?

Tenk went to speak, but nothing came out. But the caretaker was able to translate the expression on his face.

"Your man started up a party. When another guest complained, he paid for them to stay up the road at one of the big places. Then he booked every room here. Then he made some friends over at the gas station. We figured we'd let him get on with things and take our chances. We haven't been fully booked in a decade at least."

"What happened?"

"Oh you know. Music. Dancing. Naked ladies. A few bikers turned up. There were some little people – dwarves, midgets, whatever you call 'em these days – they were being thrown onto a big target. The usual stuff."

"The usual?"

"There was some fire eaters at one point. And a dance-off with your man there and a group of truckers from the pit-stop up the way there. Arm wrestling. Mud wrestling. Midget wrestling. Just your regular wrestling. Everyone seemed to have a good time and we only had to call the cops a couple of times. It all ended when your friend passed out at about 9.30."

"9.30? All that happened before 9.30 last night? He were only dropped off about 4."

"No dumbass. 9.30 this morning."

Tenk checked his watch. It was 10.14am. How was Dan not here?

"Right, I'll leave you to it. Be sure to stay again." The old man chuckled heartily as he shuffled off back to the reception booth.

Tenk looked around wondering what to do next when a gruff voice called him from behind: "Hey, are you Tenk?"

A beast of a biker with a look straight out of Sons of Anarchy was perched in a giant inflatable yellow duck with beer in one hand and cigar in the other.

"Dan said to tell you that he's gone to get Gary Tremendous…"

"No he wasn't there," Tenk began to reply, but the guy seemed to be fully clued up and waved his hand dismissively.

"Yeah, yeah. We know all that. But Dan has gone to get him. He said he's spoken to Max, crazy motherfucker, and knows what he has to do. But you my friend need to head back to England, book the venue and start selling the tickets."

"Max was here? But wait, what? For when? When am I booking a place for? We haven't got a date. We don't even know if Tremendous will come. He still hasn't been seen in years."

| 151 |

"Oh, he'll come baby." The voice was female. Tenk turned to see a traffic-stoppingly beautiful woman wearing a long white silk nightdress; the bright morning sun behind her making it almost see-through – and there was plenty to see.

"My face is up here sweetie," she said to the blushing Tenk. "He will get Gary and what Razor forgot to tell you was that the date to book is April 20th and you need to hold the event at York Hall in London, OK?"

Tenk had been working with Dan for a while now. He'd had to deal with some weird and fucked-up shit. But getting business instructions passed on through a high-end prostitute and the leader of a biker gang in a Texan motel car park was definitely up there.

"You better motor brother," said Razor. "You've only got six days to get this done."

Dan had a grin on his face like a seven-year-old on Christmas morning. He loved jet skis and he loved fast cars. He pretty much had the best of both worlds now as he stood next to the pilot of a powerboat surging out into the Atlantic Ocean. And Dan was dressed as a pirate. It had been some party at the motel, but Max had given him his mission and renewed impetus. He now knew where to find Gary Tremendous and was on his way to collect him and take him to London.

He had flown from Texas down to Venezuela, taken a ferry from the capital Caracas out to St Lucia and was now headed out to sea to the remote private island of St Graham – home to the reclusive entrepreneur who held the key to Dan reaching his destiny.

It wasn't quite what Dan had imagined. St Graham was a lot bigger than the rumours alluded to. Tremendous certainly wasn't living in a mud hut on the beach and he certainly wasn't the only resident of the island, even if all the others did work for him. There were roads, an airport, doctor's surgery, shops, a cinema. It was like a cultish commune.

Dan stayed out of sight as he made his way up to what was clearly Tremendous's mansion atop a hill – a beautiful, sprawling palace that overlooked the island and the blue ocean that surrounds.

During his journey here, he had gone through several permutations of how to approach this. A knock on the door bearing a gift? Or maybe go straight into the pitch? Hire a marching band? Pretend to be a castaway washed ashore and win Tremendous's trust over a period of days as he is nursed back to health? His train of thought was interrupted by a voice among the trees behind him.

"Can I help you friend?" It was Gary Tremendous. His face fresh and clean-shaven, his eyes a sparklingly blue and his long grey hair tied back in a ponytail. He wore casual shorts and a t-shirt. He looked like life was good.

"Ah, er, fuck, em, er, ah, shit." It wasn't quite the opening line Dan had planned. Tremendous stared at him neither in anger or amusement – just patiently waiting for this stranger on his homeland to gain his composure.

Dan took a couple of deep breaths and carefully explained to the billionaire in front of him why he was there, the journey he had taken to be there, what he wanted Gary to do, why he wanted him to do it, his deep respect for his achievements, his appreciation of his quiet life away from it all.

"But please Gary, come to London this one time. I will fly you first class, put you up in the best hotel, no expense spared. And you will be back before you know it." He put on his best smile and his heart thumped against the inside of his chest as he waited for the response.

"Listen Dan, I appreciate the efforts you've made to get here, irrespective of the apparent illegalities of them. But you would be very naive to think you are the first person to come here and try to get me to attend some event. And I'll say the same to you as I have said to them. Thank you, but no thank you. Now please leave my island."

Gary was a very clever man, but he had underestimated Dan. Dan wasn't naive at all. This was exactly one of the scenarios he had planned for and with a nod of his head, Lavernus the powerboat pilot grabbed Gary from behind and held a chloroform-soaked rag over his face.

It takes a bit longer than the films suggest, but a few minutes later he was completely out. Soon the two men were able to make their way back to the boat with their hostage. But when they got there they found it surrounded by Tremendous's private police force.

Dan thought quickly and sent Lavernus over to pretend he had just moored up to stop for a piss and would be on his way soon. With a bit of luck, they would send him on his way and he could collect Dan along the cove. But it didn't go to plan. And he watched as all 6ft 7ins of Lavernus's hulking frame was bundled to the floor and his hands tied behind his back. Could he trust his hired help to keep his mouth shut about the kidnap attempt? Could he fuck.

He was already on his toes carrying Gary Tremendous over his shoulder when the police looked up towards his hiding spot and began to charge over.

Dan had flipped from Plan A to Plan B and was now into C.

He bundled his captive into the body of the small island hopper plane and made his way to the cockpit, pulled out his smartphone and googled, 'How to fly a Cessna 172.'

With the police closing in on the aircraft, Dan flicked through the YouTube video to the 'taking off' part. He pressed buttons, turned knobs and pulled levers – and as the first bullets began to strike the fuselage, he somehow managed to rattle down the short runway and get airborne.

The small aircraft rose as it headed out to sea. Dan only said one word, but it was a long one.

"Fuuuuuuuuuuuuuuuuuuuuuccccccccccccckkkkkkk!"

ary Tremendous was in another place. White clouds. Soft white clouds. Peace. But then it became noisier. And more uncomfortable. Pain began to surge through his head as he roused from his slumber. He was in a dark cabin, but there was light streaming in from the far end. The whole place was rattling uncontrollably and the noise of engines was intense. He could make out the figure of a man in a seat up ahead. The figure now turned and seemed to be talking, but it was too noisy to hear what he was saying.

Gary tried to move, but realised his hands were tied. Only loosely though, so he was soon able to free his arms and then his legs. It had come back to him now. That big oaf on the island and his goon grabbing him from behind. But where the hell were they now?

He edged forward and as he did could start to make out some of what the man in the seat was saying.

"Wake up you fucking fuck, wake up. I don't know how to fly this thing. I don't know what's happening."

Gary leapt to his feet as everything came together in his mind at once. They were on a plane – a light aircraft – and this dimwit was flying alone. He looked out of the windows and realised they were over sea in all directions. Is this idiot trying to fly us to London?

He made his way to the cockpit and stared at the panic-stricken Dan Merriwinkle sat at the controls.

"Where are we?"

"Up! I just flew up!"

"I know up, but where to?"

"No up the map. North."

Gary looked and knew what was happening immediately.

The legend of the Bermuda Triangle lived strong in the region even if there was more than enough evidence and theories to dismiss the phenomena. But what was certain right now was that the light aircraft carrying Dan and Gary across the notorious stretch of water was falling apart. A small fire had broken out in the engine and part of a wing was flapping hideously in the wind.

Gary grabbed the radio to call mayday, but the wire had long been cut and just dangled down to his lap. The plane suddenly veered and dipped sharply and Gary was thrown against the side, his head crashing violently against a metal joint and he was once again unconscious.

Dan tried to direct the plane in the north-easterly direction. If he could just hold it out, perhaps they could still make it to England. But Dan never was very good at geography. Or physics. Or basic common sense sometimes. It was unlikely this plane would make it another ten miles, let alone 4,500. One reason was its appalling condition – another was that it was now out of fuel and plunging towards the deep blue of the Atlantic. At least he got to spend time with his hero.

Dan was not atop the clouds any more, but instead aboard a raft in the ocean. And instead of his powerful frame, he was thin and weak. He was hungry and thirsty. His clothes ragged and torn. His beard and hair long and unkempt. He looked to the floor and saw the skeleton of another man who had perished and his bones been stripped. By who? By Dan? Did he eat him to survive? Dan thought of the pulled pork burgers he had in Texas. Mmmm, pulled pork. Poor pigs. He liked pigs. And cows. And sheep. And horses. And unicorns. Unicorns. There was no unicorn riding across to save him now. But he could hear something. It was laughter. Someone was chuckling. No, not chuckling, cackling. It was a massive mocking cackle. And there wasn't just one person now, there were many. It was the exes, the bullies, the people who thought they were better than Dan. Chad fucking Kilgore. They had returned to taunt him once more. He had failed again and they were there to make sure he knew it. This wasn't a fun dream at all. Where were the gorgeous naked women? Where was the sense of euphoria and invincibility? Where had the pulled pork burgers gone? He could see images of his foes rising from the water now. They were made of water. They were coming forward to drown him. This is not what they mean by wet dream. But just then came a noise. A large ppprrrrrrrrrrrrbbbbbbbbbbb! A horn. A boat. It cut through the water enemies and made its way to the raft. Dan began to rouse; began to wake from the dream but he tried to stay with it to see who was in control of the boat. As Dan drifted in and out of consciousness, he could make out a face. Was it? Yes! It was Max. Here to save him again. A splash of cold salty water hit his face.

It was real water. Dan woke up.

I t took a moment for Dan to realise where he was. It was a boat much grander than the one in his dream. And much faster. Then the nausea hit him like a toe-punt to the bollocks and he retched over the side – the wind splattering the remnants of past meals across his cheek and beard.

He wiped it away with his hand and realised there had been a blanket wrapped around his shoulders that now fell to the floor. His clothes were damp and he felt weak. The bouncing of the boat over the waves encouraged the nausea to return and once again he was leaning over the side, screaming for Ruth.

"Slow down," Dan managed to growl from his burning throat. The pilot turned and saw the lone passenger had woken and slowed. He came over and whacked his hand on Dan's back far harder than was necessary.

"Shoe's on the other foot now fuckface." It was Gary Tremendous. He had a dried cut on his right temple and he looked a bit dishevelled, but still a darn sight better than Dan did right now.

"Where are we? What happened?"

"You crashed the plane, you dumb fuck. We drifted for a couple of days, I found help, got my boat here and that over there…" he said pointing to land in the distance "…is England. More specifically Southampton."

"What day is it? Where are we going?"

"It's April 20th Dan. I'm going to turn you into the authorities."

Fuck! Event day. At this point Dan knew only two things for certain. The first was that Tenk would not have let him down. He would've got the message from Razor at the motel. He would've booked York Hall. He would've promoted the shit out of the event and the place would be full of people expecting to witness the return of Gary Tremendous to the world of public speaking.

The other thing Dan knew was that if he did not deliver Gary, his career would be over. Back to life scrambling for the late-night discounts at Asda. Back to not being able to afford a nice birthday present for his sister. Back to going elbow-deep in stripper shit at seedy nightclubs. And he couldn't deliver Gary if he was in jail. He had to act.

Dan wasn't quite sure why there was a large wooden oar on a motorboat, but there was and it proved useful in once again knocking his hero Gary Tremendous unconscious. Even if it did take three hits. He then stepped up to the controls, pointed the boat in the direction of Blighty and gunned the engine. London here we come.

enk looked down at his iPhone and prayed that a message would appear from Dan. It had only been about 50 seconds since he sent a text to his boss, but that was just one of hundreds over the last few days that received no reply. Dozens of calls had gone unanswered too.

He hadn't known whether to alert the authorities or just follow the instructions of the bike gang leader and prostitute. He knew what he should do, but he was living in Dan Merriwinkle's world and common sense did not always apply. Very rarely, in fact.

Instead he had gone with the latter and in the process risked all he had on a mad man. The hire of the iconic boxing hall, the staff and workers needed on the day, the promotion and ticketing, and the costs of everything else needed to put on an event had gone onto now multiple credit cards. If Dan failed, Tenk would be bankrupt.

His heart thumped against the inside of his chest at that thought. Just a simple text reply would at least let him know where he stood. Especially as the doors opened to the public in 20 minutes; a queue of several hundred people having already formed outside.

"Good job T, I knew you wouldn't let me down." It was Dan! Right there in York Hall. He had made it.

Tenk was elated and relieved in equal measure. He hugged his boss. The smile on Dan's face suggested everything was OK, but Tenk couldn't get his words out.

"Where? Wha? Who? Waa? Ah? You look like shit. Where's Gary Tremendous?"

Dan led his second-in-command out to a dressing room normally used by prize fighters before their big bout. But the only person in there now had already been knocked out.

"Jesus," said Tenk. His part Irish, part Nigerian, part Spanish, part Yorkshire accent extending the word to about eight syllables. "He almost looks worse than you. What happened?"

"Well, he didn't exactly come willingly and when he said he was going to turn me into the authorities, I had to improvise."

As the pair spoke, Tremendous came to and caught the end of the conversation. Rubbing his head he said, "No you fucking idiot. I said I was going to turn you into *an* authority. I had something of an epiphany as we floated on that airplane wing and decided I would help you. If you were willing to go to that extreme then perhaps I could make a little more effort to make it easier. But then you whacked me with an oar. Three times!"

Tenk was confused and worried. Dan had gone too far. "Plane wing? You kidnapped him? Why the fuck would you do that?"

Dan's answer was simple: "Max told me to."

"Fucking Max."

Tenk had been waiting to find the right moment to broach the subject of Max for many months but had always backed out through nerves. It was, after all, a delicate subject to broach. But now his anger and frustration brought it to the surface.

"What's your problem with Max?" replied Dan, a puzzled expression on his face.

Tenk paused for a moment, contemplating the best tactic to use. He took a breath and conceded there was no 'best' way and decided to just to go with what he had planned on the flight home from Texas.

"Dan, what's your favourite country?"

"Eh? Er, the States obviously."

"OK, and your favourite film?"

"You know that: Fight Club. Epic."

"Yes, yes. And what is your favourite scene?"

"Really?" Dan had spoken about it so many times that he couldn't believe Tenk was asking. But he could also tell from his friend's expression that he wanted him to go on.

"The best scene is when Tyler Durden is holding the gun to Raymond K Hessel's head, threatening to kill him. Asking him what he wants to be when he grows up; how he wants to spend his life…"

"Go on."

"…and Raymond wants to be a vet. So Tyler says if he doesn't die that night – meaning if he doesn't shoot him dead – that Raymond should wake up the next day and go back to school and start studying to be a vet. And he keeps Raymond's driving licence and says he will find him after three months and six months and a year to check he's on course to becoming a vet. And if he's not, he'll kill him. Is this important right now Tenk? The show's about to start. I'm going on stage in two minutes."

"OK. OK Dan. So play along with me please, quickly. So your favourite film is about a guy who – hello, spoiler alert – thinks he has a partner-in-crime as it were, but it is really a split personality. They are one and the same person, right?"

"Yes."

"And your favourite scene is about this guy who is at his lowest ebb when he is forced to decide to improve his life, yes?"

"Yes."

"Dan, where were you when you first met Max?"

"Working in the strip club."

"But that very night, did anything awful happen that made you question what you were doing with your life?"

"I had to go nearly shoulder-deep into a blocked bog full of stripper shit and puke to clear it out."

"And then you met Max, yes? After closing. No one else around. And he is exactly all the things you want to be. A successful American entrepreneur with money, a nice house and opportunities and so on. And no one else has seen this guy, Dan. All we've seen is your drawing…"

"He's a private guy Tenk."

"…He has the drawing he gave you as his Facebook picture. None of us have seen what he looks like. I have seen you messaging him Dan and it looks like you are replying to yourself. And I have heard you talking onto your phone and I don't think you're speaking to anyone else. Can you see what I'm getting at here my friend? You are making great strides to becoming a real success and this event will propel you even further forward. But you are being led by a lie. A phantom. Max is all in your mind. He is not real my friend. He's all in your head."

"Tenk?"

"Yes Dan."

"Fuck off."

Dan walked out of the dressing room, through the curtain and down towards the boxing ring that would be his stage. The Prodigy's Firestarter boomed through the arena as the compere introduced him to the overly-excited crowd.

He had a killer talk planned, focusing on doing the work and whatever is necessary to achieve your goals. He had declined the offer of a suit and a shower to go to the stage looking like a castaway. After all, the tale of the last few days was one to keep the audience captivated until Gary Tremendous took to the stage.

The headline act now had risen to his feet in the changing room and was splashing some water on his face. He did care a little more about how he looked and wanted to freshen up and eat something before he went before the crowd. He was nervous too. It had been many years since he last spoke in public, but he also knew what he would talk about.

Tenk wasn't able to enjoy himself. He was still angry and confused about the Max intervention with Dan. His lecture had come out as he had planned, but Dan's reaction did not follow. Perhaps he was worse than he thought. Then something caught his eye.

Dan never went anywhere without his iPhone, but there it was on the bench. He must have left it behind when he stormed out the changing room.

Tenk checked that Tremendous was occupied in the bathroom and quickly picked it up. He knew the code and after a few taps of the keypad he was in. A pang of guilt shot through his body, but he needed to do this. He found the contacts list and scrolled down to the name he was looking for. Max. The little 2D avatar looked out at him menacingly. That grin.

Tenk took a deep breath and pressed the green phone icon, his finger trembling as he began the call.

There was silence for a couple of seconds, then it began to connect but something was off. Tenk could hear the ring through the iPhone but could also hear another phone ringing in time with it. 'Two phones,' he thought. Dan obviously had two phones – one for him and one to be Max's. He took Dan's iPhone away from his ear and followed the ringing of the other. It was coming from the bathroom.

Tenk pushed the door open just as Gary Tremendous lifted his mobile from his pocket and put it to his ear while he looked in the mirror and brushed a hand through his long, greying hair.

"Hi Dan, it's Max. I thought you were on stage."

ABOUT THE AUTHOR

GREG FIDGEON is a journalist, editor and fiction writer from the South East of England. He is married with two sons. He is 6ft 5ins tall (not wide, obviously), has tattoos and listens to loud, shouty music.

The Long and the Short Short Of It is Greg's first book. He is now working on his second - his debut novel, which is due to be completed by the end of 2017 (if he pulls his finger out).

Greg also runs a free Facebook accountability group to encourage himself and other authors and writers of all abilities. You can join at www.facebook.com/RockSolidWriters

Printed in Great Britain
by Amazon

72181207R00095